A Broken Thing

To Margie,
    Thanks so much for
listening today, and for
wanting to read some
of my fiction. I do
appreciate it.
                          All best,
                          Marlin
                          Barton

A BROKEN THING

MARLIN BARTON

FREDERIC C. BEIL   SAVANNAH   2003

Published in the United States by
Frederic C. Beil, Publisher, Inc.
609 Whitaker Street
Savannah, Georgia 31401
http://www.beil.com

LIBRARY OF CONGRESS CATALOGING-IN-PUBLICATION DATA
Barton, Marlin, 1961–
A broken thing / Marlin Barton:—1st ed.
         p.   cm.
ISBN 1-929490-20-8 (cloth: alk. paper)
1. Southern States—Fiction.
2. Problem families—Fiction.
I. Title.
PS3552.A7727B76   2003
813'.6—dc21
                    2002044000

The quotation on page 72 is from
Dag Hammarskjöld's *Markings* (Knopf, 1964).

Manufactured in the United States of America

First Edition

For

RHONDA

with love

ACKNOWLEDGMENTS

Thanks to John Tibbetts for his encouragement early on.
Thanks also to Ron Rash for his valuable advice,
and to Eleanor Lucas for her assistance.
And for unwavering love and support,
I'd like to thank my mother and father,
Jeannine Beinert and Marlin Barton, Jr.,
and my paternal grandmother,
Lillian Barton.

A Broken Thing

*B*right *streamers hang across the room. Red and green and yellow balloons with cartoon faces float among them, their ribbon tails hanging almost to the floor. Children's hands reach for them and pull. There is much laughter as the children chase down one and then another balloon.*

A cake with "Happy Birthday" written across it in blue icing sits on a table next to a punch bowl and paper cups. Presents wrapped with large bows are piled on the other end of the table. The children glance at them from time to time with wonderment and a barely concealed longing.

Young mothers sit in small groups against a wall and talk. Occasionally one will call a child's name with a hint of warning in her voice. A little apart from them, two older women sit together, talking quietly. Each of them wears a dress; the other women wear slacks. One of the older women reaches into her purse and finds a piece of candy, unwraps it, then slowly lifts it to her mouth, and a boy wearing black cowboy boots and a black cowboy hat hurries over to her with his hand held out. She smiles, reaches back into her purse, and gives him a piece of candy. "For the birthday boy," she says. The other woman pats his shoulder, then straightens his hat.

In a chair across the room a man in shirtsleeves with his tie loosened sits holding a balloon in one hand and a blue marker in the other. He turns the balloon one way, then another, drawing, careful with his work. A woman stands beside him holding a baby in her arms, and he looks up at her from time to time and their eyes meet and they smile.

The birthday boy runs over suddenly and climbs into the man's lap. "Daddy," he says, "I'm six." Then, "Can I have a balloon with a pirate on it?"

He finishes the one he's working on, hands it to a girl with long blond hair who is shyly and patiently waiting, and reaches for a large yellow balloon. He draws the outline of a face, a scarf tied around the head, then a mean frown and a patch over one eye. Above the face he draws a small pirate flag at the top of a pole. The birthday boy takes the ribbon hanging from the balloon and jumps from his lap. "It's the best one, Mama," he says. She smiles and shifts the baby from one arm to the other and kisses the baby's head.

Soon it will be time to cut the cake and open presents, then finally to take down streamers and throw away wrapping paper and paper cups and plates and plastic forks, even to pop the balloons left behind, but for now they watch the children play, listen to their laughter. The father puts his marker down and stands beside the mother. He places his hand on the back of her neck and gently rubs her there for a moment. Their eyes meet again and she smiles. Then he reaches for the child and takes it into his arms.

April–June 1974

Seth

It was gray and polished, shining almost, like a new car or something just unloaded and sitting down at the Pontiac place right in the middle of Valhia. It would have been shining as bright as any car there if it hadn't been for that big green tent without the sides that was pitched over it, and over us too, blocking out the sun, but not the heat. Roses covered the top, big red ones, but I didn't really look at them. I kept looking at the gray side of it, trying almost to see through the thing and see Grandmama lying inside, but I just couldn't see her, couldn't believe she was really in there. It was only a polished box sitting up there with a lot of people gathered around it, all of them sweating and some of them crying in the hot April afternoon.

I'd never worn a coat and tie before—it was the first time I'd been old enough where I'd had to—and I was sweating so much in them that my shirt was soaked and beads of sweat ran down my face like tears. They even tasted like tears as they landed at the corners of my mouth, only they were more salty than tears are, and more bitter tasting.

I wasn't crying. I don't know why. Mama was crying, but she wasn't loud, only sort of sniffling. My brother, who's a lot older than me, and really only my half brother—but I didn't know that until not long before the funeral, so he felt like, and still feels

like, my full brother—he was crying a little too. I didn't think
he would, but he did. Granddaddy wasn't crying. I knew he
wouldn't. He's a lawyer. I felt guilty for not having any tears, felt
like maybe I must not have loved Grandmama. But I did. I just
couldn't let go. I hadn't really cried since that day right after
Christmas.

Grandmama was always sweet to me. She carried caramel
squares in her purse, and she'd give me one anytime I asked if
she wasn't about to run out. She was diabetic and had to have
them for when her blood sugar was low. She was sick for a long
time. Her whole life really. She would sit at the desk in the
kitchen with only the one little light on above it and give herself
shots in the leg every morning. She'd let me watch. "How can
you do that?" I'd say. "I hate shots." Then she'd tell me, "It's
only a little needle. It doesn't really hurt." She'd stick herself
then. "Just a prick of the skin. I've been doing it since I was
sixteen."

The sweat kept running down me there under the tent, and the
preacher, who didn't look like he was sweating at all, went right
on talking. Only me and Mama and my brother sat with Granddaddy on the front row. There were other people in the rows behind us, and then what must have been almost all of the white
people in town crowding around the tent. It looked like hun-
dreds of people, and I thought about how everybody stands
around the big tents when a circus comes to town, only here
everybody was dressed in dark clothes and looked unhappy. I
knew Daddy was somewhere behind me in the crowd. Maybe I
couldn't picture Grandmama in the casket, but I could picture
him standing alone, and I felt sad for him.

Daddy and I had driven over from Riverfield, where we'd been
living with my other grandparents since that day right after
Christmas. We pulled up the winding driveway to Grandaddy's
house at the top of the steep hill. There were cars parked everywhere, but the first one I saw was Mama's, a little blue Chevro-

let. I knew my brother would be with her. He would have come up from Florida.

I felt nervous when I saw Mama's car because I knew Daddy would want to go in and talk to her, and to my brother, and I knew that they wouldn't want to see him. Since Christmas, I could hardly bear it when I had to see Mama and Daddy together. Even saying the words "Mama and Daddy" together sounded wrong.

There was something else, too. A week before, Daddy had told me some things about Mama, things she'd done, bad things that maybe I don't want to talk about because maybe they're things I still don't understand. And that day of the funeral, I didn't even want to think about what Daddy had told me, but I couldn't stop myself. It all had to do with those ambulances that sometimes came to the house at night.

We went inside. There were so many people that I couldn't really see anybody at first, and most of them were strangers to me. A lot of ladies with blue hair kept looking toward me and Daddy. Then Mama walked up. She had on a dark dress and she looked pretty, but she didn't look like herself. She was smiling at people with a smile that wasn't hers. It was like she wasn't really there behind her eyes. A lot of people were gathered around her, including Granddaddy and Michael, my brother.

Mama hugged me hard, and I put my arms around her, but didn't really hug her. I wanted to, but for some reason I couldn't. Daddy was standing right behind me. "Hello, Conrad," I heard Mama say over my head. Her voice was cold, and I felt sick in my stomach and even up in my throat.

Then I heard another voice say, "Hey, Conrad." It was my brother, but I couldn't believe it. He'd never in his life called Daddy by his first name. He'd always called him Daddy. I'd never heard anything so strange. Then they shook hands, like they'd never met before, like Daddy hadn't raised him.

Granddaddy came up. "Hello, Seth," he said. "I'm glad to see you." He shook my hand, like always. He doesn't hug. He shook hands with Daddy, too, and Daddy told him he was sorry about Grandmama.

"We need to straighten your tie," Mama said then, and she took me into the bedroom and sat me down on the edge of the bed. On the wall there were pictures of her when she was young. She looked about twelve or so and her hair was long and blond. I can never imagine what she was like when she was young. The pictures always seem like they must be of somebody else, like some cousin I never knew.

"I just needed to get out of there for a few minutes," she said.

"Yes, ma'am," I said. I knew why.

"Are you doing all right? Are you feeling bad?"

"I'm okay," I said.

This was almost exactly how it had been when Grandmama died. I'd been down visiting Mama in Montgomery, at our old house. She'd come into my room on Sunday morning, sat down on the edge of my bed, and asked me if I was awake. Her eyes were puffy and red, and she looked like she used to look back when she was sick all the time and those ambulances used to come.

She told me Grandmama had died in the night, and when she said it was all right to cry, tears came, but they weren't real tears. I was only crying because I thought something must be wrong with me not to feel sad enough to cry. I kept thinking, What's wrong with me?

After Mama fixed my tie and said we'd better go back into the living room where all the people were, she stood up and tried to push some of my hair into place with her hand. She did it gently, but I twisted away from her too hard. Then I saw the same hurt look on her face that I'd seen on Daddy's after she and Michael had spoken to him. I walked on ahead of her into the living room with all the old people and started looking for Daddy.

We rode to the funeral in a big black car. Me and Michael were in the backseat with Mama, and some man I didn't know was driving and Granddaddy sat up front with him. While we were riding along Michael leaned over, grabbed my arm, and looked right into my eyes. "We're going to miss Grandmama, but it's going to be all right. Do you hear me, partner?" I nodded my head. A little while before, when he'd spoken to Daddy and called him "Conrad," he'd seemed like somebody I'd never known. Now all of a sudden he felt like my big brother again, my brother who might beat on me sometimes, but who I wanted to think was always on my side.

When the funeral ended, or was about to end, I sat there listening to the preacher's closing prayer, but not really listening, not even keeping my eyes closed. I looked at that big gray polished box, still trying to imagine Grandmama inside it. Seemed like she just couldn't really be in there, about to be put in the ground. I thought about Daddy, standing somewhere behind us, alone. Everything seemed so strange. Grandmama used to be alive and asking me if I wanted a caramel square. The four of us, Mama, Daddy, Michael, and me, used to live in the same house together, and we used to eat supper every night at the round oak table in the corner of the kitchen. The white phone on the wall would always be ringing for Michael while we ate. Now everything was different, and I sat there looking at a coffin that I couldn't believe had my Grandmama inside, but it did seem like something was in there.

Conrad

I've known Laura since high school, but if you'd seen the two of us speak at the funeral, you'd hardly have believed it. Though perhaps two people can be so cold and distant and hostile only if they have known each other for a long time, shared a history that is bound by conflict. Civil wars are always the bloodiest of affairs. People divided can create a destruction unequaled by anything else, and the carnage in people's hearts can be as bloody as the peach orchard in bloom at Shiloh Chapel or that open field before the stone-lined road at Fredericksburg.

Of course now she'd say, "There you go with all that historical junk and that high rhetoric. You live in the past." She has always hated history.

After the graveside service I followed them back to her father's house. There were more people there than before, some of them already bringing food. Platters and dishes sat on the table and kitchen counters. Laura and Michael were in the living room when I found them. Seth was there too, sitting on the flower-print sofa by himself with his coat and tie still on, which I was glad to see because I'd told him he'd have to wear them the whole time. I started toward Laura, and as I drew close to her she turned and wouldn't look at me, just as before the funeral. It hurt, and what made it worse was that Seth was watching. I don't know why she didn't think about that. There I was making an effort to be decent, and she couldn't act any better. I would have expected that kind of behavior from Michael, but I'd hoped for better from her. It seemed like she might have realized how hard it was for me to come up and speak to her and offer my condolences, especially after I'd gotten that letter from her the week before announcing that she'd decided it would be best for Seth if he were with her, as if it were that simple. I'd thought everything was about at the end. I'd finally told her yes, I'll stop trying to talk you out of this thing you want, and we'd finally worked out a settlement. She'd agreed back when we first talked that Seth would stay with me. That was clear, indisputable. Now she'd gone back on her word.

"I'm sorry," I said to her, holding my anger. I knew how close she and her mother had been, how close they'd become in the last several years, both of them sick, each in her own way, and each of them in and out of hospitals. "I know you'll miss your mother. She was one of the kindest people I've known."

"Yes," she said, and that was it. She might as well have told me to go to hell.

Michael started coughing where he sat over on the stone-built hearth of the fireplace. He's had a smoker's cough since he was sixteen. I went over, and instead of turning away, he looked straight at me with such contempt that he didn't have to speak out loud.

"I know you'll miss your grandmother," I said.

"You shouldn't have come," he said. "I sure didn't think you would."

"I'm sorry to hear that," I said. "Someone had to bring Seth, and I wanted to pay my respects."

"Are you going to leave soon?"

"Well, Michael, I will in a few minutes. But maybe now isn't the time for ugly words between us."

"What do you mean? I'm not trying to be ugly."

"All right," I said, not wanting to aggravate him any further. I knew of course that his anger toward me had existed for a long time, and that it had nothing to do with my relationship with his mother.

I finally sat down next to Seth on the sofa and put my hand on his shoulder. Seth is a fine boy. The best son any father could hope for. He is my life and has been since the first moment I held him in the palm of my hand, which I did, literally. He was premature and so tiny that we thought we might lose him. His mother and I were worried beyond belief. After the doctor told us he'd finally started gaining weight, that he was out of danger, we stood there holding each other in the hospital waiting room, laughing through tears. This is history I can't forget.

I told Seth we needed to be going. He got up and hugged his mother. She held him tightly and all I could think was, He's my son and he's staying with me. Then he went over to his brother, and Michael gave him an easy punch in the arm. "Take care of yourself," he said, his tone so much softer now.

Seth was quiet as we drove back to Riverfield. He took his coat and tie off and rolled down his window as we pulled onto the highway. The wind blew his hair, and I was reminded that he needed a haircut. Somehow there hadn't been time before the funeral. I said some things to him about his grandmother to try to comfort him, but he didn't talk very much. He'd never had to deal with a death before. I hated to see him hurting, and I'd have done anything to take his pain away. He'd been withdrawn since the whole thing started back in December, but it seemed as if the week or so before his grandmother died he'd been even more withdrawn than usual. I'm not sure why. Perhaps it was because of the talk we'd had about his mother and the things she'd done.

I've always wanted to be a good father. Other fathers spend all their spare time playing golf or tennis or occupied with little hobbies. Why aren't they with their children? Taking care of my son is my first duty. Not that I think of it as something I have to do. It's something I want to do. That's why he had to stay with me. His mother wasn't able to care for him as well. She'd had problems—emotional, mental, whatever you want to call them—and when I got that letter from her, I had to tell Seth those things about her, about the hospitals and why she was in them. She left me no choice.

As we drove along the highway that afternoon after the funeral, I put my hand over on his shoulder again. He closed his window after we'd gone a few miles. His hair was blown all out of place, and when I took my hand and tried to smooth it, he jerked away from me.

May

Seems like you always want to cook when someone dies. You hear the bad news, and you just go straight to the kitchen. It's something to do, I guess. You feel like you're helping in some way. Usually you send food over to the family, but of course I didn't feel like I could do that. So that night I put all my time into cooking for my grandson. There was fried chicken, fresh snap beans and cream corn, and cracklin' bread. All the things he likes.

We ate as soon as Conrad, Sr., got home from the store. He pulled up in his truck about six-thirty or a little after. Seth sat at his place beside me at the dining room table. He didn't eat much, and he sure didn't say much either.

"How was the cracklin' bread?" I said to him when we were about done, just to get him to say something.

"It was good."

"I was afraid the cracklins got too hard."

"No, ma'am. They were fine," he said.

We all kept sitting there in the quiet for some reason, even though we were finished eating. Then I remembered something I had to tell Seth. "Bobby called for you this afternoon," I said. Bobby is one of the boys who live down on the Black Fork River, right off the Loop Road. His daddy and Son used to play together when they were little, but later they, well, drifted apart.

"When did he call?" Seth asked.

"About four o'clock. I told him you were at the funeral. He said maybe he'd come by tomorrow after school and y'all could go down on the creek."

"Yes, ma'am," Seth said. He wasn't talkative, but at least he was well mannered. He went on back to his bedroom after he got up from the table.

"Maybe seeing Bobby will help him feel better," his grand-daddy said.

I felt so for him. He looked like he hurt as bad as any boy ever had.

We were afraid we were going to lose him, and we just couldn't allow that. It was simply out of the question, no matter what had to be done. Sometimes hard choices have to be made and we made them. I don't regret what we did, or what I did.

But that night I didn't have much time to worry about things. I had dishes to wash and two more loads of clothes to get finished. Seth needed a ripped seam in a shirt sewed up. Son came into the kitchen late and wanted to talk, but I had to tell him I had too much to do before bed. Things couldn't wait because Conrad had told me he needed me in the store all day the next day. I was just too busy to talk. Taking care of a family is a big job, and it was something I hadn't had to do in a very long time. But one must do what has to be done. You have to sacrifice and not think about yourself. Laura never understood this.

I got to bed, late.

"You get everything done?" Conrad said from his side of the room.

"Yes. Finally."

I turned my little light on and read my Bible for a few minutes. It always helps. All I have to do is pick it up and read wherever it opens to. That night I think I read Psalm 51. God's word will always lighten your load and restore you. After reading I placed my Bible back on the bedside table, turned off the light, and said a prayer for us all then, especially Seth, and I didn't forget to pray for the soul of his grandmother, who I always liked and admired. She read her Bible too. And then, because I suddenly felt it in my heart, I prayed for Laura, letter or no letter.

Seth

We walked quiet along the bank, checking out each little hole as we came to it. Minnows and bream darted back and forth in the shallow water. We looked for snakes, cottonmouths. There are always a lot of them down on Granddaddy's creek. We only had pellet guns, not .22's, but Bobby said if we could shoot enough times, we could kill one. Mussels were dug in along the sandbars, and their shells stuck up out of the sand just below the surface of the water. I'd used their insides for fishbait. Bobby had showed me how to pry them open with a pocketknife. He said crickets worked better, if you had enough money to buy some down at the Bait Shop. I couldn't imagine not having enough money for crickets.

I'd known Bobby before we moved to Riverfield. I'd played with him some when I used to come up and visit, but it was after we moved and I started seeing him at school in Valhia that we really started doing things together. Everybody made fun of me for a long time because I was from Montgomery and because I didn't know things like the difference between a sweep and a plow. I wasn't a country boy. But Bobby would come by the house to see me even though he had to ride his bike four miles to do it. He lives down on the Black Fork in a place called Duffy's

19

Bend, which is off in the direction of Demarville, another town about ten miles away.

The creek took a sharp turn, and we came to the big sweet gum behind the old house where Daddy was born and raised. A robin sat on one of the lower branches, and Bobby lifted up his pellet gun, took aim, and shot. He missed, which wasn't usual for him when it was so close. We'd gone after birds a lot that spring, and he could always hit them. He motioned for me to take a shot. I raised my gun, but I missed too.

We walked the rest of the creek, but didn't see a snake. Bobby wanted to go look for more birds.

"Why don't we go right across y'all's pasture fence into those woods?" he said.

"That's the old part of the Methodist cemetery," I told him.

"That don't matter," he said. "I'll bet there's lots of birds in there."

We crossed the fence. The woods were dark and thick with a lot of vines and brush growing, so it was hard to walk. Underneath all that brush old gravestones were hidden. Most were from back in the 1800's. Bobby didn't want to stop and look at the dates, though. "Come on," he kept saying. He wanted birds.

We walked a little farther, and Bobby stopped suddenly and shot a sparrow out of a pine tree. Then I saw a blue jay in an oak and took careful aim this time. It fell hard to the ground.

"Good shot," Bobby said. "Now we've both got one."

We came up on a little cleared-out place in the middle of the woods. I'd been looking for it. It's where our old family plot is. Daddy had showed it to me a few years before. He always keeps the plot good and clean. My great-grandfather and great-great-grandfather are buried there. I know all about them. My great-great-granddaddy fought in the Civil War under Forrest and Fightin' Joe Wheeler. Daddy had read up on all that, and he'd told me about some of the battles my great-great-granddaddy was in, like Seven Pines.

20

I told Bobby that these were my family's graves, and we sat down on two of the headstones. It was cool in the shade of the trees, and the stones were cool to the touch. It was peaceful. The day before I'd been at my grandmama's funeral, and now here I was, sitting in a graveyard, but I liked it. I thought about Grandmama and suddenly felt like maybe I shouldn't even be out with Bobby, that it wasn't right, that maybe I should have been home and feeling sad for her.

"Let's go," Bobby said. "This place feels spooky."

"All right," I said.

After we got back to the house, I wished we'd stayed in the woods. Two people waited on us outside in the yard. One was Bobby's sister, Frances. She had on a dark blue shirt that fit kind of tight, and you could see she was big up top. Her light blond hair was getting long. It was halfway down her back. After Bobby and I closed the pasture gate, Frances walked toward us.

"Hey, Seth," she said and smiled at me like she wished she could think of something to make me blush. "Bobby," she said, "you got to get right home. Daddy sent me for you. Says you got work to do. Says you shouldn't have gone off."

"All right." Bobby walked to the old blue truck that Frances was driving. Then he shot the last pellet in his gun up at a pine cone. "I'll see you later," he said and got in the cab. Frances waved to me over the steering wheel. She cranked the old truck and backed away, and I wished I could have gone with them because there, over in a chair beside the carport, sat my brother, and something about him didn't look right.

"Have you seen Daddy?" I said. Then I noticed that Daddy's car was gone.

"No, I haven't seen your father yet." He stayed in his chair and watched me. His eyes were little slits, and he looked at me like I was dangerous or something. He'd said "*your* father." It sounded mean.

"He must not be here," he said and laughed kind of quietly,

like there was some joke or secret he knew. "Thought I'd surprise him," he said. "But it's you I really came to see. What's wrong? Don't you want to see me?"

The way he talked made me nervous. I felt like he was telling me some kind of a lie, but I couldn't figure out what the lie was.

"So how are you doing?" he said.

"Okay. I've been shooting my pellet gun." I held it up.

"Who was that girl?"

"Just my friend's sister."

"We had us a nice little conversation. She's got a nice ass, doesn't she? She said she liked you."

I didn't say anything.

"I saw you looking at her when she was walking toward that truck."

Yesterday he'd finally talked to me like we were brothers. Now he sounded just like he did when he'd first spoken to Daddy, except this time he was talking to me.

"Why don't we go inside?" he said, and he started to get up, but Daddy came pulling into the carport about that time. He got out of his car and looked real surprised to see Michael.

"I didn't expect to see you here," Daddy said, "but I'm glad you came."

Michael didn't act like he was going to get up from the chair, but he finally did. They shook hands again, just like at the funeral, only this time Daddy took his other hand and put it on top of both their hands. Michael didn't pull away like I thought he might. He kept on shaking and shaking until it was almost as bad as if he *had* pulled away. He kept staring at Daddy.

"Are you testing my grip?" Daddy said.

"No. I'm just shaking your hand. That's all. Can't I shake your hand?"

Michael finally let go and sat back down. Daddy leaned against the car.

"How are things for you down in Florida?"

22

"Been working my ass off," Michael said.

I stared down at the ground, then looked up. Michael had never cussed in front of Daddy, but Daddy surprised me. He only nodded his head.

"A little hard work never hurt anybody. What are you doing?"

"I'm on a tugboat," he said. "We pull boats." He put a cigarette in his mouth and lit it with a silver lighter from his pocket. He'd never smoked in front of Daddy either.

"Can you tell me what kind of work you do on the tug?"

"It's just work. That's all. Like anything. We pull one boat, then we pull another."

"Okay, Michael," Daddy said, and it sounded like he'd suddenly decided something. "How's your mother today?"

"She's all right."

"Good."

I wanted to say something, but nothing came in my mind, and even if it had, neither of them would have heard me, seemed like.

"Will you be going back to Montgomery with your mother?"

"Yeah," he said. "Tomorrow."

"Good."

Michael took the cigarette he'd been smoking, and even though it was only half gone, he threw it down on the carport. The smoke from it drifted up toward Daddy. He hates cigarette smoke. Michael didn't crush it out, neither did Daddy. They both just looked at it.

"Seth, why don't you take Michael here around the yard and let him have a turn with your pellet gun? I bet he'd love to shoot something." After he said that he went on inside.

Michael got up, and I handed him the gun. He pumped it up a few extra times, and we started walking. It's a big yard, about an acre, and a lot of pines grow around the house, so we started looking for birds.

"I killed a blue jay today," I said.

"That's good," he said and took a shot at a pine cone. The gun made a louder noise than usual because Michael had pumped it too many times. He shot a second pine cone and this one fell. "Where your grandparents?" he said, pumping the gun back up.

"At the store."

It shouldn't have surprised me to hear him say "*your* grandparents," just like he'd said "*your* father," but it did. It sounded as strange as him calling Daddy "Conrad." Then I got to thinking how he'd never spent much time with me here when we'd come up to see our grandparents. I'd never thought about it much before, but he'd always stayed in Valhia. Now that I knew Daddy wasn't his real daddy, it made sense.

Michael didn't shoot anymore, and he didn't say much. It seemed like he got bored, and then he handed me the gun and started walking back to Mama's car. He was leaving already, but he stopped first and lit another cigarette. Then he looked toward the house a minute, like he was waiting for Daddy to come out.

"Do you want to go in before you leave?" I said. "Or maybe we could take a ride."

"No, I guess not." He turned away. "No," he said again, only this time it was sharper. He got in the car and shut the door. The window was rolled down, but he didn't say anything else to me or even wave good-bye. He didn't feel like my brother at all.

After he pulled away, I went inside. Daddy sat in a chair in the living room looking out the big picture window. He hadn't heard me come in. "He's gone," I said.

"Well, I'm glad he came by to see you, that's good." He kept staring out the window. It was like he wasn't even in the room, like maybe he was back in Montgomery with all of us sitting at the supper table or watching television in the living room or getting ready to go somewhere. I put my hand on his arm, and finally he looked up at me and put his right hand on top of mine. His hands are big. The wedding ring he used to wear would fall off my finger, even off my thumb. Sometimes we'd play a game where I'd try to touch the palm of his hand and pull back before he could grab my hand in his. He always got me, and I couldn't get out of his grip no matter how hard I pulled and twisted. His hand was like a vice. Finally he'd let go. Then I'd want to do it again. Each time he'd grab my hand I'd get frustrated when I couldn't pull out of that iron grip of his. I'd wish I was as strong.

Michael

Iwas fucked up. And by the time I got back to Granddaddy's house in Valhia I was even more fucked up. Mama came out of the house and was standing under the carport when I opened the car door.

"Where have you been?" she said.

I got out of the car. "Went to see my brother," I said, then stumbled, but caught myself real quick. Not quick enough though.

"Are you drunk, or stoned?" she said.

"I only had two beers, that's all."

She looked at me and shook her head back and forth. "I guess you were that way when you went to see your brother. What a fine example you always set."

I slammed the door shut and looked her right in the eye. "I didn't have but two beers, and that was after I got back. That's the truth."

Always lie when you have to, I say, and stick to the lie no matter what. If you tell somebody the sky was green yesterday and say it enough times, I mean say it over and over and over, not only will they start to believe it, but so will you. That's the secret. Believe your own lie. So if Mama had asked me, "Did you do any downers before you saw your brother?" I'd have told her, "No, I

26

did not do any downers before I saw my brother," and that would have been the truth because I would have heard myself say it and then I could believe it. And when I told her I went to see my brother, that was the truth too, and I believed it just as soon as I heard the words come out of my mouth. So if she had said, "Did you go there just to aggravate your stepfather?" I'd have said, "No, I did not go there to aggravate my stepfather," and that would have been the truth too, and I would have believed it.

"You're just like your father," she said. The sun shone under the carport, and she had to cover her eyes with her hands to see me. It looked like she was putting on a mask. "The second you hit puberty you became him," she said. "You walk like him, talk like him, lie like him, smile out of the corner of your mouth like him. And you haven't even seen him since you were four years old."

Now *she'd* told a lie, and she'd told it real well because she believed it was the truth. But it wasn't. The truth is that I'd seen my father two years before, and had seen him since then, too. But she'd told the lie so well, because she'd believed the lie, that for a minute I believed it too, believed that I hadn't made those trips to Selma and seen the man who was my real father. I didn't want to let her know that I'd seen him. So I had to believe her lie (which she didn't know was a lie), if just for a minute. Sometimes you've got to believe someone else's lie to help your own. It all takes practice.

I didn't like her talking about my father. She'd told me a long time ago that she never wanted to hear his name again, and I'd wanted to tell her that I didn't want to hear another bad thing about him come out of her mouth. My father's a good man. He served his country. He owns a business. He supports his wife, even if she's only his common-law wife. She doesn't work, except maybe to serve a beer or two in his place on a Saturday night when the river people come in off the Alabama.

I found out he owned that bar in Selma from my grandfather, who let it slip, and I decided it was time to see him. I remembered him from when I was four, but he was kind of like a dream in my memory. Still, I'd never forgotten him. I made the fifty-mile trip and walked into his bar on a Saturday afternoon. Weren't many people in there. Both the front and back doors were propped open to air the place. It needed it. It's not exactly plush. I recognized him from an old picture—he looked older, but he's still a handsome fellow and I do look a lot like him I'm proud to say. We're both tall with brown wavy hair, deep-set eyes, and strong chins.

I sat down at the bar and told him to pour me a draft. He looked at me for a long minute. Hell, I thought maybe he'd figured out who I was. "Let me see some I.D., buddy," he said. I got it out, and he looked at it. "You ain't old enough." I told him, "Maybe you better take a closer look." He stared at me. "You some kind of a smart ass," he said. I got nervous. I'd been pretty cool about the whole thing, but I started sweating. A couple of flies buzzed around some spilled beer on the bar, and there was a hot breeze from the old black fan that hung from the ceiling. "Maybe you could take a look at the name," I said. So he looked again. He'd recognize my last name. He'd known Conrad.

He started nodding his head a little. "You said you wanted a draft?"

So I drank a beer with my father, my own father. The two of us sat there like men. He didn't talk much at first, but finally, after a lot of beer and after I told him I could remember him, he said a few things about my mother. Said he never could make her happy. No matter what he did, it was wrong. She finally just ran him off, he said. He didn't want to leave her, or me. That's exactly what I heard him say, "I didn't want to leave," and I believed it. You better know I did. I heard the words come out of his mouth.

Before I left, he asked me how I'd made the trip from Montgomery. Told him I'd hitchhiked. "Here," he said, "if you're hitchhiking, you'll need this." He reached under the bar and handed me something for the trip back home. Never mind what it was. Just something my father gave me. I kept it with me wherever I went until it finally got lost. Well, not lost exactly, but that's close enough.

It was almost dark by the time I walked out the door of the bar. Streetlights were starting to come on. They were making that humming noise you hear after night starts coming and they first click on. I was pretty drunk, but I found my way back to the bus station, handed my round-trip ticket to the driver, and soon we were headed back over the old Edmund Pettus Bridge with the Alabama beneath us.

Mama didn't know about any of this. I knew better than to ever tell her. When we finally walked into Granddaddy's house from the carport that day, she was still going on about how much I was like my father. I turned to her in the entrance hall and said the one thing that I'd always wanted to say. "So do you hate me as much as you hate him?"

That shut her up. She looked like I'd hit her in the stomach. I said it and left it said. She went to her room and didn't come out for a while.

That night she fixed some sandwiches for supper, and the two of us sat down at the table and waited for Granddaddy. Mama was sitting real stiff, and I know she must have rehearsed what she said to me. I guess she wanted to get it right. "Michael," she said, "I don't hate you. I'm sorry for the things I said. You do remind me of your father sometimes, but there is one important difference, you're my child and I love you." When she said that I could only wonder who she was trying to convince. But she kept right on going. "I found that I didn't love your father," she said. "There were reasons. He wasn't a good husband, and this may hurt you to hear, but he wasn't a good father. It wasn't in him. If I hadn't been practically a child when I married him—and I've told you how young I was—maybe I could have seen these things."

"He never really got the chance to be my father, did he?" I said. "You had to leave him and then you married somebody else."

She looked down at her sandwich again, like now that her speech was over she didn't know what to say. But finally she looked up at me and took a deep breath before she spoke. "That's right," she said. "Instead we had Conrad, and no matter what you might think of him he never stayed gone for days at a time or cheated or drank or ran up debts."

I didn't say anything else. All I know is, and I'll say it over and over and over again, Conrad was never a father to me. He didn't take me places. And when I got older he started riding my ass all the time. I'd come home and he'd want to know where I'd been. Why was I so late? Was I high? He never trusted me. That time I ran away with my friend from school, after Conrad found us, he wanted to put me in reform school. Mama didn't want to do it, but he pushed for it, and you better believe I went. Two weeks in jail. Let me tell you, there were some tough guys in that place. I didn't have to go in there. You think he'd ever put Seth in a place like that? Hell no, not in a million years.

There's only one man who's been anything like a real father to me, and that's my grandfather. He can be hard as nails. I know that. He was hard on Mama when she was growing up. But when I was little he'd take me to his law office or over to the probate office, or take me around to see pieces of property he wanted to look at. He took time with me when nobody else did. And if I'd wanted to go to college, he would have sent me. Not that my grades were ever anywhere near good enough. I never studied.

That night, he finally came into the dining room and sat down with Mama and me at the table. He must have heard some of what we'd been talking about. Before he took a bite out of his sandwich, he looked over at me. "You listen to the things your mother is telling you, Michael. And don't ever let me hear you speak to your mother that way again. Do you hear me?"

"Yes, sir," I said and then started to eat. I'd do anything for that man. And that's the truth.

Seth

That afternoon I walked back down to the creek and watched the muddy water go by. I threw sticks in and pitched rocks at them, trying to sink each one like they were battleships or something. So much was on my mind, though, that after a while I didn't really pay any attention to where the rocks landed. I finally jumped the creek and walked up the hill, then crossed the fence and in a minute or two found the little open place in the woods and sat down against the stone marked "Rafe Anderson," my great-great-grandfather. Bobby had said the place was spooky, but the trees and vines made shadows that were nice to hide in. I started to think about things that I didn't really want to think about, but it was like I couldn't stop myself. The stillness and quiet were too much.

I'd been asleep in Michael's old room that morning after Christmas. He'd moved out the summer before, headed for Florida. Daddy had said headed for trouble. His room was bigger than mine, so I took it. It had a double bed too. We used to wrestle on it. Sometimes he'd hit me, too hard, and Daddy would get mad at him and tell him not to do that again. That morning after Christmas I woke up all of a sudden. Something was wrong. I don't know what it was that told me. I didn't even think about going out and riding the new bike I'd just gotten, even though it was the ten-speed I'd been wanting. My heart beat fast, like I was afraid someone was going to come in my room and beat me worse than Michael ever did. I wanted to get up and see what was wrong, but I couldn't.

The shower was running in the bathroom across the hall. Maybe that's what told me something was wrong. It didn't make sense. Michael wasn't home, and I was the only other person who ever used that bathroom. I could tell it was late in the morning by the bright sunlight in my window, and both Mama and Daddy should have been up and dressed. I should have been hearing their voices. Then I remembered that they'd gone out the night before with some other people. I could tell Daddy hadn't wanted to go because he'd had kind of a mad look on his face, like when I don't do something he's asked me to. They got back late. I heard them come in and heard them talking to the girl from down the street who'd stayed with me. Everything had seemed all right then.

I kept listening and heard the shower cut off, then heard Daddy clear his throat, so I knew who was in the bathroom. I opened my door, and that was scary too, like someone might be standing on the other side, waiting to hit me in the face when I stuck my head out. I walked out into the hall. The bathroom door was closed and Daddy was still in there. I went and looked in my old room and the bed was messed up. It's happening, I thought.

Daddy came out of the bathroom, wearing his robe and slippers. He motioned for me and walked up the hall and into the den, then sat down on the sofa. I followed him and sat beside him. He looked tired, like he'd been working all night.

"Your mother's still asleep," he said. He sat there, staring off into the room, but not looking at anything. "Your mother and I aren't going to live together anymore," he said finally. He took my hand. I started crying, but in a way it was a relief to hear the words. The fear I'd had for so long about what might happen—

the fear I'd felt because of the way they'd always talked to each other, or *not* talked, the way they could sit in a room together and neither one of them really be in it—all that old fear was gone. But as I sat there I started to feel scared all over again. What was going to happen now? Where would I live? What was going to happen to me? Then Daddy said, like he'd heard what I was thinking, "You and I will be together, of course. You don't have to worry."

In a little while he got up and went to get dressed. I walked back to my room, Michael's old room, shut the door, and lay down on the bed. I wished Mama was up and would come in while Daddy was gone. I didn't want the two of them to come in together. There was a knock at the door after a while. It was Daddy. He walked in and sat down on the bed. "It's going to be all right," he said again. First there was just a wet shine in his eyes. Then he had to wipe tears. He'd never cried before, and I kept trying to think of something to say. I wanted to help him, but didn't know how. He was hurting, and his tears hurt me.

Mama suddenly stood in the door, all dressed, with a suitcase in her hand and a purse on her shoulder. She was looking at Daddy, but started talking to me. "Seth," she said, "get dressed and come walk out to the car with me." She didn't say anything to Daddy.

I put some blue jeans on, and a shirt, and found her in the living room. "Do you want me to carry anything?" I said, not knowing what else to say. She just shook her head.

"Where are you going?" I said. It was hard to believe that I had to ask her a question like that. How can you not know where your mother is going when she's got a suitcase in her hand?

"I'll stay with some friends for a few days," she said. "Don't worry."

I followed her out to the car. She put her suitcase in the trunk, then slipped her sunglasses on and bent down toward me. Her glasses were bright green and they hid her eyes. Then I thought something strange: A color can be as thick as a wall. "I'm sorry about what's happening," she said. "I know there are lots of things you don't feel like you understand. But I want you to know that I love you very much." She hugged me and I put my arms around her, but I kept looking back toward the house. She held me for a long time, and I could feel her whole body shaking finally. Then she let go and got in her car and pulled away down the street. I still didn't know where she was going, and I couldn't tell you now.

As I sat there on the grave marker in the cool of those woods, I kept thinking about how Mama left that day, then about how I'd acted toward her at the funeral. And I thought about the ambulances that used to come to the house, too, the way those men would carry her out.

Laura

They all thought I was crazy: Conrad, May, Mr. Anderson, even the doctors. For a long time I believed them. I thought I was crazy. But it was not insanity, it was depression, and the only insanity was what was done to me. A sort of desensitization one doctor called it. The worst of it was the piece of black rubber. It tasted like some dead and hardened flesh. I'd know what was next, and that short moment between the first taste of rubber and what came was true horror. For those moments maybe I did go crazy.

Sometimes I felt as if they were all trying to drive me mad, and when I got better, strong enough to see what I had to do for myself—leave Conrad for one thing—they tried again to make me crazy by taking my child from me. But I was never crazy, they were, and I decided I wasn't going to lose my child without a fight.

On Wednesday night, not too long after the funeral, I was trying to read but couldn't make the words mean anything. Then the phone rang, and I answered after the second ring and heard the word "Mama." I've always wished that Seth and Michael would call me Mother, but that night "Mama" sounded wonderful. "Can I come see you this weekend?" Seth blurted the words out before I'd even said hello. I was shocked. I'd felt him slipping away from me since that first day after Christmas. I'd told Conrad to wait until I got up so that we could tell him together. But no, he didn't do that. He had to start working against me right away. The hell with how it all might affect Seth, but I know that he didn't think about that. Only a mother would think about that.

I worried about the things his father was probably saying to him about me, especially after he got my letter. He would have told him every terrible thing he could think of, all to turn Seth against me, and the worst of it was that he wouldn't have had to lie. It was as if Seth were about to fall from my grasp, fall down a well with deep water at the bottom, and I just couldn't hold his hand tight enough to stop him. Sometimes, though, it was as if I were the one who was about to fall. Or perhaps I should say fall again. I'd already fallen as far down as anyone can go, down into my own well, and swallowed so much water that I'd almost drowned. After the funeral I was beginning to wonder just how many losses a person can stand. My mother, who I'd come to find out was stronger than I'd ever known, had been someone I'd leaned on. Now she was dead. Michael was slipping away too, into his own confused world. And even though it was something I'd wanted, Conrad was gone, and there were times in the middle of the night when I walked around the house that used to be a home to all four of us and stared at the empty rooms that I'd think, I've made a mistake.

On the phone that night, all I said was, "Of course you can come."

So on Friday afternoon I left the law office where I've worked as a secretary for ten years and picked Seth up at the bus station down on Lee Street. He had a new gray suitcase in his hand that looked too big for him. When he walked through the glass doors from the terminal, the thick smell of diesel fuel followed him.

"Where'd you get the new suitcase?"

"Grandmama got it for me yesterday."

37

"Let's get out of this bus station," I said. "It smells in here."

We went out to eat before we went home. I'd decided I'd take him somewhere nice, so we went to the Elite, one of the few restaurants left downtown. I ordered a steak for him, and I got fish. After the waiter left, there we were sitting across the table from each other and suddenly it was just as awkward as it had been the day of the funeral, only now I couldn't tell myself that it was because Conrad was constantly there in the room with us. But perhaps in a way Conrad *was* at that table sitting between us. Perhaps the things he must have said to Seth about me were just as much a presence as he had been at the funeral. By the time the waiter brought the bread and the salad, I was furious at Conrad for what I'd imagined he'd done, but I kept my composure. After all, it wasn't Seth I was angry at. How could anyone be angry with a sad, scared twelve-year-old boy? And perhaps I was wrong. Maybe his father hadn't told him anything. But I doubted it.

"How are things at your new school?" I said.

He looked up from the piece of bread he'd been cutting. "It's hard. Harder than my old school. Grandmama helps me with all my homework every afternoon."

"How long does it usually take?" I said.

"About three hours. Sometimes longer."

"That's too long."

"Grandmama says that after I get caught up it won't be bad, and that I'll be able to do it by myself. She says that I'm just going to a better school now."

"What else does your grandmother say?"

"What do you mean?"

"Nothing. Never mind," I said.

The meal finally came, and he told me about a friend that he'd made.

"Do you have other friends?" I said.

"Well, not really. Not close ones."

"What about at school?"

"I know people there now," he said, "but some of them aren't too friendly."

"Some things never change," I said. "Valhia isn't a very friendly place. I grew up there, so I know. You give it some time and you'll make one or two good friends."

I realized as I spoke that my own child was having to tell me about his life. Something seemed so wrong in that. Nothing that had happened since Christmas made sense anymore. He was telling me things that I should have already known. I suddenly felt a deep guilt. I'd wanted to leave Conrad, not my child. But I'd known that I might have to sacrifice them both. When I got up from the table and told Seth I had to go to the rest room, he gave me the same surprised look that he used to give when I'd have to leave the supper table because I couldn't hold back tears. So often, back then, I'd start crying, hardly knowing why. At least that night I did know why.

After we got home we sat and watched television together. Then I told him he had to go and take a bath before he went to bed. He kept saying he'd go in a minute. Finally I told him no more putting it off. He pouted a little. "March, young man," I said, and for the first time since he'd walked in from the bus terminal, I felt like a mother.

While he took his bath I went to his room to unpack his new suitcase. It was locked. I was puzzled at first. He'd been in it since we'd come home because he'd walked into the bathroom carrying his pajamas and tooth brush. Then I knew. When he finally came back into the den to tell me good night, I told him to sit down. He took his father's old chair.

"I was going to unpack your suitcase for you, but it was locked," I said. "Can you tell me why it was locked?"

He looked down at his lap and started to play with his hands.

His hair was wet and little drops of water ran down his neck and forehead. "Grandmama told me I ought to keep it locked, that she bought it for my trip to see you because it had locks."

"Seth, you know you can trust me, don't you? All I wanted to do was put your things away so you wouldn't have to do it."

He didn't say anything. He only kept his head down.

"Do you have anything in there you don't want me to see?"

He shook his head.

"You have to trust me, Seth. Can you? Can you trust me?"

He began to quietly choke back tears, and I went over to his chair and kneeled down in front of him. He reached out and held onto me. His still-damp hair felt wet on my neck. If his grandmother had been in that room, I would have torn her to pieces.

That night I dreamed of buses. One after another was pulling out of the terminal downtown, each making that terrible racket. They were all empty, but I knew that Seth was on one of them, and I ran after each one, shouting for the drivers—who I couldn't see—to stop. Finally a bus did stop and a driver stepped out. He wore a cap and dark sunglasses, and somehow looked like a villain from a bad movie. "Where's my son, you son of a bitch?" I said. He slowly opened the baggage compartment underneath, and the smell of diesel fumes came pouring out in a cloud. Seth lay sprawled across the suitcases, and I grabbed him out of the smoke and fumes. The odor of the diesel fuel had saturated his hair and his clothes. "I'm sick, Mama. I'm sick," he kept saying. That heavy smell of diesel was somehow the most frightening part. It was as if it had filled his body and was coming out through the pores of his skin.

So I wasn't really prepared to deal with what I saw in the den the next morning. Michael lay stretched out on the sofa. I'd forgotten that he still had a key.

"What are you doing here?" I said.

"That's not the kind of greeting I was hoping for from my own mother."

"I'm just surprised. Are you all right? Has anything happened?"

"Do you mean am I on the run from the law?" he said.

"No, that's not what I mean."

"I'm all right. I just decided to come for a visit."

"When did you get in?"

"About an hour ago."

"Seth's here," I said.

"He is?"

"He decided to come about as suddenly as you did. Come on in the kitchen and I'll fix you some coffee," I said.

Later I went to wake Seth up. He was asleep in his twin bed. "Seth," I said, "your brother is here." He opened his eyes, and I went over to his bed, sat down, and leaned close over him. As strange as this may sound, I think I did it so that I could check to see if he smelled of diesel. There was only the slight scent of soap on the freshly washed sheets.

After Seth got dressed he came into the kitchen, sat down at the table, and said hello to his brother.

"How's it going?" Michael said. "Expect to see me again so soon?"

Seth smiled, but I wasn't sure what to make of it. I didn't know if he was glad to see Michael or not. He somehow looked suspicious of his brother.

"It's good to have the both of my boys home," I said, and as soon as I did I realized how true it was. Here were my boys sitting at the table eating bowls of cereal, like Saturday mornings used to be. Then I realized both of them would be gone soon.

Before we even left the table Michael got a phone call, and he went out a little before lunch to "go meet someone." How anyone knew he was home, I didn't know. I wondered if he'd been in Montgomery for several days, and if he had, why hadn't he at least called? I thought something might be wrong. If he wanted to tell me, he would. There was no way my asking him again would have done any good.

I took Seth to a movie that afternoon. It was some adventure movie about a boy lost in the wilderness, and it upset me because I made the obvious connection. Later we walked around Oak Park and went to the planetarium there. We stopped for ice cream on the way home, and while we sat at the cement picnic table in front of the place, I thought, None of this is right. These aren't the things I do with my son. I don't take him to parks and planetariums. I make him clean his room. I make him do his homework. He felt the difference too, I think. On the way home he didn't talk very much, and once we were in the house he went to his old room and didn't come out for an hour or so. At one point I stopped and looked in. All he was doing was lying on his bed throwing one of his brother's worn-out baseballs up in the air and catching it.

Michael didn't come home that evening. I'd hoped he'd spend some time with Seth, but he hadn't come in by the time Seth went to bed, and he still hadn't come in by the time I fell asleep.

The next morning was almost a repeat of the day before. I woke up early, about six o'clock, and walked into the hall. I wasn't going back to sleep so there was no point in trying. At least I hadn't had any bad dreams. None that I remembered. Seth's door was closed, which was strange, and Michael's bed hadn't been slept in. I cursed. He'd stayed out all night. But when I looked up the hall I found Michael on the sofa again. I walked into the den and saw that this time he was asleep—sound asleep. I wondered why he hadn't gone to his bed, and then I went into the kitchen. An empty pint bottle of whiskey sat on the stove. I pulled the garbage can from under the counter and threw the bottle in. It made a clatter against empty beer cans. If it had been only one or two beers, and if the empty bottle hadn't been there, I wouldn't have minded.

I picked up the bottle out of the garbage, took it into the den, and dropped it on Michael's stomach. He didn't wake. I stood there for a minute, then began to smell just the slightest hint of that sweet, sick kind of odor that I used to smell in his room and finally learned was marijuana. "Get up, damnit," I said. "Get up." He came to and blinked several times before he really looked at me. "Who do you think you are to come into this house and do what you've done? How could you do this?"

"Do what?" he said.

"You know what."

"I just meant to have a couple. Guess I went a little overboard," he said.

"A little overboard? You shouldn't have done this, especially with your brother here. Did you want me to see all of this? Did you do this to spite me? Obviously you did. And what kind of drugs did you have? I smell the marijuana. Were there pills, too? What goes on in that head of yours? What? Tell me!"

"I don't know," he whispered, then rolled his eyes.

"Did you take pills, too?"

"I might have. I don't remember," he said. "What if I did?"

You think he would have lied and said no, as good as he is at lying—just like his father. Maybe he was still too drunk to think about lying.

"You can't come in this house and do these things," I said. "You'll have to leave."

"You're throwing out your own son?"

He's always had a flair for the dramatic.

"Yes, I am. Whenever you think you can come back and not bring drugs and alcohol into this house, you'll be welcome."

He just stared at me. My hands shook, and there was that empty feeling in your stomach you get when you haven't had anything to eat and you feel faint. Then I heard the front door open and close, and Seth walked into the room. Just what is going on here? I thought. It's six in the morning. He shouldn't have been out.

"Wait a minute. Where have you been?" Seth stopped and turned around. "I want to know what you've been doing outside this early," I said. My voice must have been still full of anger from talking to Michael, but I was more surprised to see him come walking in than anything else. I know he heard anger, though. His eyes were opened wide, and his mouth hung open as if he were waiting for words to come out.

"I just went outside," he said. He looked toward his brother, and their eyes met for a moment. There was something going on. "I woke up early, and I just wanted to walk up my old street."

"I don't believe you," I said and then regretted it as soon as I spoke. He was all right. I could see that, and there I was, scaring him, maybe even driving him further away from me. The two of them looked at each other again. "Something has happened here that y'all aren't telling me about. What is it?"

"Nothing," Michael said. "And that's the truth."

"Go on to your room, Seth," I said. He walked down the hall. Then I turned back toward Michael. "A lie. I'm sorry," I said, "but you're going to have to leave. There's no other way."

I went back to bed, curled up under the covers, and all I could think was, I've handled this all wrong. I've made a mistake, just like my sending him to juvenile hall was probably a mistake. Conrad tried to tell me it was. He tried to talk me out of it. Now here I've scared one child and thrown the other out. What in God's name am I doing?

My head began to hurt. A migraine was building. I can always tell. When I first started having them, back during all my hospital stays, the doctors told me that I didn't *really* have migraines, that I was making them up and that's why my head hurt and my body ached.

Later in the morning I heard Michael go into Seth's room. They argued. Then I heard the front door slam. Michael had gone. I'd hoped he would talk to me. I'd even imagined him coming in to apologize and ask if I was all right.

Seth came in not long after his brother left. "Are you having one of your headaches?" he said.

"Yes. How did you know?"

"I just thought you might be."

"I'm sorry I yelled at you. I was angry at Michael, not you."

"It's all right."

"You'll have to fix yourself a sandwich for lunch," I said. "I'm going to have to stay in bed for a while."

That afternoon I finally got up. I still hurt but could move around, and Seth had to get to the bus station. His father would be waiting to pick him up. He was already packed with his things beside the door, and seeing his suitcase all ready to go hurt worse than my headache. I felt that his seeing me sick in bed all day must have made him think of all those other times when I was sick. I'd frightened him again.

I drove him downtown and waited inside with him. We sat on those hard plastic seats and listened to the ringing sound of the pinball machines behind us that seemed to grow louder and louder after each boarding call.

"Things will get better, Seth," I said when there was a moment's lull in the noise. "I'm going to make sure of it. I promise."

I couldn't make sure of anything, though. My promise was a lie, but I wanted to believe it.

His boarding call came. We walked out into the terminal and hugged good-bye. His brown eyes looked as sad as I felt. He walked up the steps, carrying his suitcase, and disappeared behind the dark-tinted and dirty windows. After the door slammed shut, the air brakes hissed and the bus backed away, then pulled out of the terminal. I was left standing alone and watching the cloud of diesel exhaust that built behind the bus. Its smell reminded me of something dead.

At home that night, with my children gone from me, the house empty and quiet, I felt afraid almost the way a child feels afraid, a child who perhaps has lost its mother. Those old words "motherless children" kept coming into my mind and I thought, I am one of those now, even at my age. My mother is dead. I won't see her again. Then there was the question, Will my own child be without me? Will he be motherless? I remembered that there were times when he almost was, and I felt guilty for that too, and so ashamed. But that is in the past, I thought. That won't happen now.

Late in the night I got up out of bed and went to my bookshelves. A year or two before I'd put away one of Mother's letters in one of my books. It was the letter I cherished most, and I needed to hear her voice, needed to be close to her. I unfolded it, took it to bed, and read it over and over, and did not think about the hour of the night.

Emily

Dearest Laura,
I've been lying awake for some little time and finally realized that mentally I was "composing" a letter to you, so I thought the best thing to do was to get at least some of it down on paper. I don't know really what it is—an impulse, I suppose.

I know that you are having problems with Conrad, and it occurs to me that he and George (it seems right to speak of your father as "George" here) are much alike. We so often marry men who are like our fathers. I say "we" because I find so much of my father in George. And I suspect that you see your father in Conrad. But George, even at his worst, is not the hard man my own father was.

Memories of hurt can come so suddenly. I'm remembering now the day the army came to the door and told us brother Chet had died of influenza. This was in 1918. Father had told Chet if he joined the army, he could not come home again, that he was no longer a son. It was Father who answered the door that day. We didn't know who was there. Father came back to the table where we were eating, sat down, put his napkin back in his lap,

47

and said, "Chet's dead." He started eating, and we all knew not to say a word, not to leave the table. Perhaps one reason I'm telling this story again is because the first time I told it to you, when you were a teenager, you looked at me with such empathy, and I knew for the first time in your life you looked at me not as your mother, but as a person, a friend. And now, years later, because of our troubles, I feel that the friendship has grown in a way it couldn't then. You were too angry at me in those years. Angry for my not standing up to your father for you. I'm sorry that I didn't. I was fighting so hard for myself. But I don't mean to make excuses. It seems to me that you and I have long forgiven each other our failures.

I know that right now you are suffering terrible loneliness in your marriage, and I wish so that I could say something that might help you, but I don't know how without making it all sound trite. All I can say is that I know you feel tremendous barriers between yourself and Conrad, but don't let those barriers turn back toward you and enclose you in a place where you are completely sealed and might feel there is no way out, save for one dark lane. You have to find life for yourself in the space you make and hold onto that space. I know whereof I speak.

I hope these words make some sense to you and that they *don't* sound trite. I'm not sure of many things at all, but I'm quite sure that I can say anything to you without being laughed at. I'm not afraid of that with George exactly, but with other people I guess it has been the great fear of my life. I feel blessed that I have a daughter like you who I can talk to and write to. A true connection between people is so rare, even between mothers and daughters. I think a lot about my mother's life, and how much easier mine is than hers must have been. She never complained, had, ultimately, much more courage than I have, and yet didn't have a daughter's understanding. Whatever understanding I might have has come too late for her. It is that lack of connection that is so tragic. So I am deeply appreciative of you, and hope it can be the same for you with your boys.

I love you very dearly.

Mother

Seth

The bus back to Demarville, where Daddy had put me on, wasn't too crowded, but there was that same old smell, like all the seat cushions were dirty from people's sweat. By the time we pulled out of Selma, I'd started thinking about Mama and all that had happened. The worst thing was after Michael came. But I took care of everything. Mama didn't need to know all that went on.

I woke up about one o'clock that night and went to the kitchen to get some water. Michael was sitting in the den in Daddy's old chair with the lamp on low. He was drinking. I'd never seen him drink before, but I knew he did. He did other stuff too. The room smelled funny.

He didn't pay much attention to me after he saw I wasn't Mama.

"What are you doing?" I said.

He just took a drink from his beer can, real slow. His eyes were only about half-open, and he stared real hard out at nothing. I walked toward the kitchen, and when I got close to him I saw the pistol in his lap. He wasn't holding it in his hand. It was only lying there. It was a small automatic. I knew about guns. Daddy had already taught me.

"What are you looking at?" he said. He sounded like he'd

been to the dentist and had his mouth shot full of Novocain. His words just fell out of his mouth.

"Michael, where'd you get that gun?" I said.

He picked it up in his right hand and rested his elbow on the arm of the chair so that the gun was pointed toward the ceiling. "My father gave me this gun. I went to see him. Before I left, he said, 'Here, you'll need this.' I carry it everywhere, partner."

He started waving it around while he talked. He couldn't hold it steady. His finger rested on the trigger, but the hammer didn't look like it was cocked. Still, I was scared. He kept waving it past his head and even stopped and rested it flat against the side of his face. He dropped his beer can out of his other hand, and beer spilled all over the floor. I ran to the kitchen, got a towel, and went back and got down on my knees and started mopping it up.

"Why didn't you bring me another beer?" he said.

"Don't you think you've had enough?"

"Goddamnit, no I don't think I've had enough. All that's left is the beer. Go get me one. And who in the hell do you think you are to tell me what I need or don't need?" He waved the gun again. It was pointed my way some of the time. "You're not my father. And I'll tell you something else, your father's not my father."

"I know that."

"Well you didn't used to know. All those years, you didn't know."

I kept mopping up the beer.

"If you don't get me another beer, I'll get up and get one myself."

"I'll go," I said.

I rinsed the towel in the sink and then got his beer out of the refrigerator.

After I got back and handed the beer to him he pulled open the top and took a big swallow. There was still a small puddle of beer at his feet, so I got down and used the towel again. When I looked up at him the beer can was between his legs, and he had one hand over his face and the other still held the pistol pointed toward the ceiling. He started talking again, real quiet this time, and he was even harder to understand.

"This is the only thing my father's ever given me," he said. "The only thing. Your father, he gave you whatever you wanted. But my father, this is all he's given me." He waved the gun around and then put it in his other hand and looked at it. He was crying, and I got *real* scared. There was no telling what he might do. "All I wanted, all I wanted . . ." he kept saying, but he didn't finish.

"Let me see the gun, Michael," I said, but he acted like he didn't hear. He started crying harder, way harder, than he had at Grandmama's funeral. I didn't know what to do.

"I don't have anything but this," he said. "Nobody gives a shit about what I do." He looked right at me then.

"I do," I said.

He shut his eyes for a second when I said that, like he was really trying to believe what I'd told him, and before I knew what I was doing I'd grabbed the gun out of his hand. He opened his eyes real quick, but before he could grab for me or the gun, I ran down the hall and into my room. He didn't come after me. I guess he figured he'd wake up Mama, and besides, he probably thought he could get it in the morning. But I didn't take any chances. I hid the pistol in my suitcase and locked it, then put the key under my dresser. He wasn't going to get it again.

By in the morning I'd already decided what I'd do. I woke up early, put on my clothes, and got the pistol out of my suitcase. I was afraid Michael would be awake, but when I walked through the den and into the kitchen, he was sound asleep on the sofa with his mouth wide open. I walked out of the house with the pistol in a garbage bag I'd gotten from the cabinet above the stove. At the end of the street there's a real deep sewer hole, and I dropped the pistol through the widest part of the rusted grate.

It was wrapped in the bag still, and it hit the bottom and made a little splash. I knew Michael would kill me.

When I got back to the house, Mama was in the den hollering at him, and she went after me too, a little. She was so mad, but I wouldn't tell her where I'd been. I couldn't.

Later on, Michael came into my room. "Where is it?" he said.

"Where's what?" I was hoping maybe he'd been too drunk to remember what I'd done. I'd seen on television that sometimes when people are drunk they can't remember things later.

"You know what I'm talking about. Where's the pistol?"

If I could have thought up a lie, I would have told one. "I threw it away when I went outside," I said.

"You little son of a bitch. I ought to beat the shit out of you. Goddamn you."

"Go ahead," I told him. I was mad then, just like him. "I don't care. I thought that gun was going to go off last night and kill you. I don't care what you do to me." But of course that was a lie. He stared at me, and I stared right back at him. I'd never done that before.

"Where'd you throw it away?"

"I'm not going to tell you," I said. "But even if I did, you couldn't get it."

"You little shit," he said. "My goddamn father gave me that pistol." He grabbed my arm and punched me hard in the shoulder, then shoved me back down on the bed. But that was all. I thought he'd keep hitting me.

In a little while he left with all his stuff packed in a duffel bag. He didn't even tell Mama good-bye. He gunned the engine in his car and flew out of the driveway like he didn't care what might have been coming down the street, even if it had been a little kid on a bike.

I went in to check on Mama later. She had one of her headaches, but by that afternoon she felt good enough to take me to the bus station.

After I got back home, I didn't tell anybody about what had happened. I just didn't want to worry or upset anyone, especially Daddy.

The next day I looked forward to seeing Bobby at school. Maybe I wanted to tell him about Michael. I don't know. How do you talk about something like that? But Bobby wasn't at school, and I felt a little lost without him there.

That afternoon, I told Grandmama I didn't have any homework, which was a lie. I had to go down to Bobby's, but I didn't tell her that. I pulled my bike out of the shed and pedaled hard down the Loop Road toward Duffy's Bend. The whole time out there on that quiet road I kept thinking about Michael and what he might have done with the pistol.

There was an old black truck with Georgia plates parked in the drive at Bobby's house. I knocked on the door and Frances opened it. "Come on in," she said. "Bobby's got a sore throat, but you can still see him." Then she said, "We've got company. Mama's brother."

I followed her into the living room, and the whole family was in there: Bobby, his brother Johnny, their mama and daddy, and their company.

"Come on in, Seth," their mama said. This was only about the second time I'd ever seen her. She sat on the sofa with a green bottle in her hand and had a big smile on her face. She's got a streak of gray that runs through her hair and makes her look kind of like a skunk. Their daddy was on the sofa, too, wearing an old brown cap, and he was listening to the man sitting on the stool in the middle of the room. Bobby and Johnny were both sitting on the floor, and I went over and sat by Bobby.

"What you doing?" Bobby said.

"Nothing. I just rode down."

"This is Uncle Dan," he said, pointing. "We all call him Mighty Man." He whispered so he wouldn't interrupt.

Mighty Man was real small, and wiry too, and had black hair

that he wore slicked back. There wasn't anything about him that looked all that mighty. He didn't take any notice of me, but kept turning his head from the television to Bobby's daddy. He held a green bottle in his hand like the one Bobby's mama had, and he kept drinking from it real fast. One of those black dance shows was on. "Look at those niggers jumping up and down on there," Mighty Man said. "Look at that one there, kicking his leg out. Shit. Bunch of niggers. I swear."

"You shouldn't carry on so, Mighty Man," Bobby's mama said. Then she turned to Frances. "Go get Mighty here another Green Devil and bring him that plate of food I warmed up in the oven. Mighty's got to keep up his strength for when we put him to work in the garden after a while."

"Like hell," Mighty Man said. "I'm going to sit up here where it's cool and get drunk off my ass."

Bobby's mama laughed.

Frances came back in with the plate and the Green Devil, and Mighty Man took them and set the bottle on the floor and the plate in his lap. He picked up the fork, looked at it like he was studying it, then looked at all of us. "This fork's dirty," he said. He held it out for all of us to see. Then he lifted his left arm, put the fork right in his sweaty underarm, clamped down on it, and pulled the fork out. He took a look at it again, studying it. "There, that's better," he said, and started eating.

"You're sick, Mighty Man," Bobby's mama said. She was laughing again. "Mighty, this boy sitting beside Bobby, he ain't never seen nobody like us. And I know he ain't never seen nobody like you."

What she said made me a little mad. She was right, though. They were like nobody I'd ever seen, even though Mighty Man reminded me of Michael that night in Montgomery. Still, he was different somehow. He was drunk, but he was laughing. Michael hadn't been laughing.

Then all of a sudden Bobby's mama said something strange. "I bet his daddy and his grandparents don't like him coming down here. But I bet they don't say nothing, and you know why. It's not just because we drink sometimes, either."

"Hush!" Bobby's daddy said under his breath and gave her a mean look.

I didn't know what she was talking about, but it scared me somehow.

"Come on," Bobby said. "Let's go back in my room."

We went to his bedroom and Johnny, who's two years younger, came with us. We played checkers for a while. Bobby said his mama wouldn't let him go outside because of his throat. After a few minutes Frances came in and sat on the bed with us and watched us play. She was right beside me, and she put her arm on my shoulder and kind of leaned against me. It made me feel nervous, but it was nice. Then she took her other arm and put it across Bobby's shoulder.

We played a good many games and talked some about school and about fishing. We kept hearing Mighty Man and their mama laughing. Finally I said I'd better go. I could see that I wasn't going to get a chance to tell Bobby about my brother. I got up and so did Bobby and Johnny. Frances lay back on the bed and stretched out. She looked pretty with her soft blond hair all over the pillow. When I turned toward Bobby and Johnny I saw a strange thing, or at least it seemed strange. There was a mirror in their room, and we were all standing in front of it. Bobby and Johnny are both kind of small in size, and the mirror hung just right for them to see into it, but I'm taller and the mirror wasn't right for me. What I saw looked like a picture where somebody's head has been cut off. It was like I just didn't fit in with them at all. About that time I heard Bobby's mama. "I believe you scared that boy," she said to Mighty Man.

"What boy?"

She laughed again.

I rode my bike home and looked out at all the pastures and

plowed fields and old run-down houses where black people live. They sat out on their porches, watching me pedal by. Skinny old dogs ran around their houses, and a little kid walked out onto a porch without any clothes on. I thought about Montgomery then. All the streets had rows and rows of nice houses, like ours, and the yards were always mowed. But I didn't live there anymore, and at the same time, I didn't really feel like I lived here. Nothing seemed like it made sense anymore. Nothing felt like home.

Conrad

After Seth had been home a few days, I tried to find out something about his trip. He lay on his bed with a hunting magazine, but he didn't appear to be doing anything more than looking at the pictures. I asked him about his mother, if she was all right, and then if he had seen Michael. First he said that he hadn't seen his brother, but he changed his mind. "Well, he did come while I was there, but he didn't stay long," he said.

"Why not?" I asked.

He closed his magazine and studied the picture of the white-tail deer on the cover as if he were trying to memorize its every detail. "I don't know. I guess he wanted to see some of his friends," he said. He didn't look up at me when he spoke.

"Had he been back down to Florida, or had he not gone yet?"

"I don't know," he said, still studying the deer.

I know my son. He wasn't telling the truth. Something had happened down there that he felt he couldn't tell me about. I didn't know if it had to do with his brother or his mother or both of them, but something had happened. I worried about him having to go back to Montgomery again, and it was that night when I finally wrote the letter to Laura that I'd been trying to write for a week. I told her Seth could not possibly live with her, that I could not let that happen. It simply wouldn't be the best thing for him.

I spent the next several evenings working in the store, waiting on customers and bagging groceries, something I'd told my father I wanted to start doing. It helped to take my mind off Laura and what she might do next. I feared her reaction, but during the day I stayed too busy to think about her very often.

I'd started a new job. In Montgomery I'd been an assistant administrator at a nursing home for a number of years. Back in the fall, an old classmate of mine had let me know that there was a position open for a chief administrator at the nursing home in Demarville. He'd recently been made a member of the board. I hadn't pursued the position because Laura didn't want to move. What I wanted didn't matter to her, of course. But then everything changed at Christmas, and I knew that I had somewhere to go. It meant a move up, which was important.

My new job kept me occupied, but Seth had me worried. One night toward the end of the week I sat up late with my mother even though I'd been through a long day of board of health inspections. I told her that something must have upset Seth during his last visit.

She leaned toward me. "I think so, too," she said. "He went off on his bike the other day and didn't tell me where he was going. He said he didn't have any homework. It's not like him to act that way. To just go off. To tell a lie."

She looked at me for a moment, as if she were waiting for her last words to sink in.

"I don't like his going to see her," I said.

"Do you think you should let him? You don't have to. Fight her. Think about what's best for him."

"I always think about what's best for him."

Later, I went to bed and, because I had been having trouble sleeping, I decided to read. I took up a volume about the battle of Sharpsburg and read until the early hours of the morning. It was one of the bloodiest battles in the war. Lee was far outnumbered, but he had the highest ground and did terrible damage. Afterward, though, he left the field and took his men back to Virginia. Because of this most of the histories will tell you it was a Northern victory, but as far as I can see the South won. Yet as I read I thought that somehow it made sense that such bloodshed would not make for clear victory.

Finally I went to sleep and dreamed the most vivid of dreams that I could recall. I was a child again, looking out the open front door of the old house across the pasture where we lived then. My father was standing on the long front porch. He looked so much younger; and even though I stood there as a child, I thought, He looks like me, like the grown man that I've become. For a moment it was as if I didn't know who was who. Then I saw my mother standing out in the yard, and she was about to turn away from my father and toward our front gate, as if she might be headed toward the store, but I wasn't sure. Something wasn't right. I felt as if she might *not* be headed to the store. She looked so much younger, too, and she was pretty—a thing a child never realizes about his mother. Neither one of them moved. They just stood there fixed, my mother half turned toward the gate, my father standing on the porch. Then I noticed an odd thing: my mother held a large purse in *each* hand. But they were really too big to be purses. Suddenly it was morning and the sunlight was coming through my window in dusty streaks and warming the room. I realized then that it wasn't just a dream I'd had, it was a memory, one that I didn't particularly want to recall. My mother had been about to leave my father, and me. I never knew why.

By the end of the following week, I found out what Laura would do next.

I was at home alone on Saturday. My mother and father were both at the store. Seth was down along the creek. I heard someone at the door, and when I opened it, I was so surprised to see

Laura's father standing there that I didn't know quite what to say. He was dressed just as if he were about to go to his office.
"May I come in?" he said and took off his hat.
"Yes. Come in," I said with some reluctance.
We walked through the kitchen and into the living room and sat down. I kept looking at his briefcase.
"I want to talk about Seth," he said. "About this hard line you seem to be taking."
I felt all the muscles in my arms and chest tighten then.
"Can't you rethink what you're doing?" he said, as if *he* ever would.
"There is absolutely nothing to discuss," I said. I spoke the words sharply, just the way I knew he would have said them.
"I'd hoped we could at least talk about it."
"No. I'm surprised you would think that," I said, then realized that he probably did know better, which left only one reason why he'd come.
He took a breath and looked at me, then reached down for his briefcase, sat it in his lap, and opened it. "I'm afraid I'm going to have to give you this, then," he said.
He handed me what I knew was a subpoena. I felt my face tighten into a stone mask, and I stared at him hard enough to make most men turn away. My hands and arms began to shake with anger, and I found it hard to breathe. "Leave," I said. It was all I would risk saying. I was afraid that if I spoke again, even one more word, we might get into a shouting match. If he'd been anyone else, a younger man, someone who wasn't my father-in-law, I don't know what I might have done. There have been times in my life, times I don't like to remember, when my anger has grown almost beyond control.
I followed him outside and watched him leave. He got into his black Cadillac and slowly drove away. Then I sat outside on the back porch, trying my best to calm down.
Seth finally came through the pasture gate, chained it shut

again, and walked toward the porch. When he got close he looked up at me oddly and started to speak, but something made him stop suddenly. He seemed to think better of saying anything at all.

"What is it?" I said, perhaps too sharply.

"I think I'll go out to the barn for a while," he said, then walked away quickly. I didn't see him again until his grandmother came home and called him in for a late lunch.

May

Ididn't tell anyone I was going. I knew that I'd be back before
Seth got home from school, and both Conrad and Son were at
work. So I got in my car and went, just like that. It was time for
me to see what I could do.

There weren't any cars in George Tyner's office lot, but as it
turned out, there was one Negro in the waiting room. I told the
secretary who I was and sat down. I didn't have to wait long,
only a few minutes. A Negro came out of the main office, and the
other one went on in, then came out after just a bit. They were
probably both paying rent on houses Mr. Tyner owned.

Then I marched in. Mr. Tyner stood up from his chair behind
the desk and said hello. He sat down after I did. He had on a
nice-looking suit and his hair was combed just right. In other
words, he looked like himself.

"First I want to say how sorry I am about Emily. I hope you
got my card," I said. I had to be sure to get that out.

"Thank you, May. And yes, I did get your card," he said. "I
appreciated it."

"I don't want to take up your time, so I'm going to get right to
the point. Don't you think maybe Laura is doing a foolish thing,
that she'll only end up hurting herself, and everyone else. I think

deep down you know this, and you should stop her, or at least try. It would be what's best for all."

He waited a moment before he spoke. "I don't know that, May," he said. "I don't think she'll be hurting anyone."

I started in again, a little harder this time. "She won't be a good mother to Seth. She thinks she will, but she won't be. She doesn't understand what it means to put others before herself, doesn't know what it means to sacrifice." I paused. "That she's been a failure as a wife and mother ought to be clear. You remember when she swallowed all those pills at my house—while her own child was right outside?"

"Now wait a minute, May. You're talking about my daughter here. And Emily's," he said, which I somehow felt like I'd forgotten for a moment. "I won't have it in this office. Not for one minute more."

"Well it's true. I've made sacrifices. I've put my family ahead of myself. I'm doing it now."

"Who are we talking about here, May? You don't have to take care of Conrad and Seth. It isn't your responsibility."

"Yes it is. And I'll do it as long as I have to. I learned how a long time ago."

He didn't say anything more to that, and I went on again about how foolish Laura was being. I kept telling him that he had to stop her, and he just kept saying, "I won't do that," over and over in that lawyer-like tone, like I was a child and couldn't understand plain English. I got more angry each minute. I couldn't help thinking about Son, what losing Seth would do to him. "All right," I told him, then took another pause and a deep breath and got ready to say the thing that I'd been afraid I'd have to say. "We'll make Seth hate his mother. We can do it. We'll have to do it."

He looked like I'd hit him in the face. "You had best leave now, May," he said. He meant it. His face had turned red and he was about to lose control.

I did leave, but took my time. I walked back through the waiting room, spoke again to the secretary, and went on out the door.

On the way home I had to make myself keep slowing down. My Pontiac will really go, and I could hardly stop myself from mashing the gas pedal to the floor.

Laura

It started with Seth, as strange as that may sound: an ending beginning with a birth. After Seth was born Conrad would go into his room when he got home from work, pick Seth up from his crib, and look down at him and say, "You are my life now." Those were his words, and there was something in the way he said them that scared me. He somehow meant them too much, if that's possible, and I think it is. He would spend hours in that room with Seth, just the two of them. I would be busy cooking. Often it would get dark on them because Conrad would forget to turn on a light once the sun had gone down. I'd go in right before supper was ready, and they would be two shadows in the dark, like ghosts or something. They felt that far away from me, that untouchable. Then I'd turn on a light. Neither one of them would look up. "Why don't you bring him into the kitchen with Michael and me, instead of always staying in here?" I'd say. He'd answer "okay." He never did.

But sometimes Conrad would pass the doorway to the kitchen on his way to Seth's room and stop and look in on Michael and me for a moment. Michael would be sitting there quietly at the table, and his eyes would suddenly come alive with a second light. He'd wait for just one word from Conrad. Then he'd have to watch as Conrad turned away and walked back down the hall to Seth. Michael would grip the table top with his small hands and stare at the empty doorway, as if Conrad might reappear if he wished hard enough. Michael wouldn't say a word, and if I spoke, he'd hardly answer. Sometimes he'd go outside and throw a ball against the side of the house. I'd hear one hollow thud after another. They sounded like blows to a body.

Maybe Conrad spent so much time with Seth because we came so very close to losing him when he was born, and there had been all the health problems afterward because Seth was eight weeks premature and was still developing inside. He'd be in pain and crying, even after we brought him home from the hospital, and Conrad and I would go to him in the night and try to quiet him. Once Conrad looked at me almost in tears. "My son is hurting," he said, "and I can't do anything for him." No, you can't, I thought. Those were bad nights for both of us, but Seth turned out fine, just as the doctors had said he would. Now, though, I think of all the hours we spent with Seth, *both* of us while he was healing, and I can only imagine what must have been happening inside Michael.

As Seth grew bigger, as he grew out of wearing only diapers and into baby shoes and baby clothes and then into children's clothes, Conrad became less a husband and more and more a father, *only* a father, the kind who tries to keep such constant watch over a child that he becomes like a guard, one who stands always at a careful and disciplined attention. If Seth were playing outside and fell, Conrad would pick him up almost before he hit the ground. At night I'd feel Conrad getting in and out of bed as he constantly went and checked on Seth asleep in his room.

So often fatherhood is what finally makes some men become men, but maybe there are others who are simply ruined by it. And when the child of one of these fathers grows older, into a teenager, maybe a girl who sneaks around with an older boy, maybe one who's already joined the army and says he wants to marry her, even though she's only fifteen, then these fathers are no longer guards who protect the child. They begin to keep watch as if over an inmate.

So there I was, five years into the marriage, in my early thirties, with two children and a husband who seemed to be changing in ways I couldn't understand, but which were somehow familiar. I would be doing the dishes, seeing my reflection in the dark glass of the window above the sink, and remember how my father would come in from the office in his suit at night and begin to question me as I sat in the kitchen with my mother. "What did you do after school today?" he might say. But it wasn't asked in the way most parents would ask. He wanted answers, specific ones. If I told him my friends and I had gone walking down past the depot, he'd say, "It's not safe there. Don't go there again. Do you hear me?" Or, when I was older, thirteen maybe, I might tell him I'd gone for a ride with some older girl, and he'd say, "She drives too fast. She's too old. Don't go anywhere with her again." I learned not to tell him certain things, but he'd find out and there would be punishments. He wouldn't let me leave the house for weeks, except for school. He wouldn't let friends come over. But it was his disapproval, the way he would look at me, as if to say, "You have failed me. You are no good," that hurt the worst. As I got older, fourteen, fifteen, it seemed that all I got from him was disapproval, and not the one thing I needed most, what all girls need from their fathers. He finally made me start working in his office every afternoon, where he could keep better watch over me.

But it didn't work. I married Michael's father, secretly, at fifteen, and after a year passed, he asked me to come join him where he was stationed up North. I walked to the bank that day and asked the teller to withdraw all my money. When I turned around my father stood there wide-eyed with his hands on his hips. Once we were home, I told him I was married, and that I was leaving to be with my husband. I didn't let him stop me. And later, when I asked him to handle the divorce, he said "no." He told me that I'd made a decision no matter how young I'd been and that I had to learn to live with that decision. He did not change his mind. He did not forgive.

These were the memories I began to recall as I washed the supper dishes and listened while Conrad sat at the kitchen table and asked Seth what he'd done all day. I'd see my reflection in the dark glass again and I'd think, He is still here, in this kitchen. You haven't gotten away from him. You tried getting married to a scoundrel who drank, cheated, and ran up debts. You sat there while the furniture and then the car were repossessed. And now look at you, standing here in this kitchen, remembering the man you thought you'd gotten away from.

Maybe it wasn't fair of me to compare them in their seriousness and their rigidity. Maybe they weren't so much alike. But that's how I saw them—my husband and my father.

Then the depression came. I don't know when it started. I can't give you an exact day or month, not even a time of year, but it came. If one can inherit the tendency, then I probably did. And from whom? My father. Who else? He's never spoken of his depressions, but now that I'm older, now that I've had them, I recognize his times of brooding for what they were. Now I know why he would sit in his chair in the den for hours with the lights off.

I think I was depressed for years maybe and didn't even know it. It can happen that way. It can be so slow, the way it builds. As Seth got older I was often tired, yet I couldn't sleep very well. And all the demands made on me as a wife and a mother and as someone who worked everyday were more than I could handle, but I did handle them. I kept the house clean, cooked, went to the grocery store, spanked Seth when he had to be spanked (Conrad wouldn't do it) and restricted Michael when he got too old for spanking and worried myself sick when he began to get into more and more trouble. I showed up on time for work and took dictation and typed letters and brought home my check. I did all those things May said I failed to do, goddamn her! I did them like everyone else, and I did them well past the time I saw any reason for doing them, or for doing anything. I was tired. I wanted rest.

I began to imagine not going home right after work, just walking down deserted streets for a few hours maybe. Then I read *Anna Karenina* and even imagined getting off work and walking through downtown to Union Station. I wondered what the cool metal tracks would feel like against my face. Later, as I got worse, as I began to lose all hold and perspective, I would shut my eyes when I got in bed at night and feel my body begin to fall—spinning, my stomach turning—fall farther and farther until I hit water, and I would feel the perfect blackness below its surface where it was warm and quiet, just so quiet, so peaceful.

I began to imagine taking a handful of sleeping pills, imagined choking them down with a single swallow of water. I stopped taking my one pill every night and started saving them up, hoarding them. I was getting ready. No more thinking, or even dreaming about it as I sometimes did when I slept.

Conrad and I were hardly talking at all now. We'd had separate beds for several years. Each night I'd cook supper when I got home, and after the four of us ate, I'd clean up the kitchen, then take a bath. Afterward I would sit in bed and read. On weekends I'd go to the library and get more books for the next week. I read the Russians, and philosophy. I was searching, trying to find sense in books at a time when nothing seemed to make sense. Sometimes Conrad would say, "Do you have to read quite so much? Can't you talk to me? I know you're depressed. Can't you let us help you? You have a family."

Then one night, a Wednesday night, I did not read. I sat in the den and watched television. Conrad was in his chair on the other side of the table and lamp between us. Michael and Seth were on the sofa, arguing. It was about nine o'clock. The drugstore had delivered more sleeping pills that evening after supper. I'd called in the refill when I first got home. Conrad was there with me in the bedroom when I phoned. I don't know why I called. I had more than enough.

Maybe that night I sat there thinking about all those pills I had hidden. I can't remember. I only know that I got up from my chair with my glass of water and walked down the hall and into the bedroom, didn't say a word to anyone as I left. I changed into my nightgown, then got the pills out of the drawer in the bedside table. It was as if I were taking my usual one to help me sleep, the way I used to, only it wasn't one this time. I swallowed them all, then lay back and began to feel myself fall, farther and farther, past all reason, past everything.

I never hit the surface this time. I only awoke, which had its own jarring. A nurse stood over me, and my stomach and throat felt as if they had been pulled inside out.

After that there were doctors. Conrad spent all the evening hours with me during that first stay in the hospital. He looked down at me one night. "What can I do? Tell me," he said. And I thought, It's just like the time Seth was a baby and sick with pain. You can't do anything. But I didn't say it. I didn't want to hurt him.

There were other times after that. There's no need to tell them all. Ambulances and sirens and orderlies and doctors ("Do you feel like talking today?"), and nurses and straps and pieces of black rubber ("Please bite down hard"), two children at home ("Why can't you come home? You don't look sick"), and a husband worried sick, a husband who didn't know what to do so he let the doctors do what they wanted, let them do it time after time after time, until he finally said "No. No more electricity. No more. No. And no more pills." For that I am thankful to him.

Getting away from the doctors and the hospitals gave me a kind of freedom, I think. I no longer had to worry about the cure. I only had to worry about the sickness, and there was relief in that, relief in the sickness. Just sickness. One can get well from

71

sickness, I thought. It is possible. But I had Conrad asking me, over and over, "What can I do? Just tell me." And I began to think, Go away. That's what. Just leave. But I felt such guilt then. He had worried and sat beside me, and all I could think was, If you don't get away from him, you will never get well. And yet, how would I find the strength to tell him to leave? or find the strength to be a person again, a mother to the one child who was still at home?

Then mother sent me a quote. So much came from her that I'm only now beginning to realize. There were her letters, her love of words and writing, and her own example of how to live. But the last real gift was that quote, those words I read. I don't even know what they were from. "*Yes* to God: yes to Fate: yes to yourself. This reality can wound the soul, but has the power to heal her." And when I read that I thought, Yes. Just that. Yes. The words didn't make me well. They only made me believe I could get well, made me remember *again* that one can get well from sickness, and that was enough.

So finally, after months of believing, I told Conrad what I wanted, told him what he could do for me. We were sitting across from each other on our beds; and he looked at me, his face blank, but not surprised, and said, "No, that can't be what you want. You're not well. Wait. Wait and see how you feel when you're well."

And so I waited, but not long—a month maybe. The second time there was a darkness in his eyes that I had seen only when he was very angry, those times when I'd yelled at him a little too loudly, had pushed him a little too far. It was a frightening look. And that night, sitting on the edge of my bed, I saw it again. I did not push. I let it go and waited. Another month. Then I knew I had to push. I'd made up my mind. We were in our bedroom again, the door shut. "All right," he said, "I'll give you what you want, but you won't have Seth. I mean it. You won't. I won't let you. I'll have my son with me."

"He needs me," I said.

He leaned towards me. "Never." His eyes had taken on a darkness again, deeper than I'd seen before. "I'll kill you first," he said.

The words were hard and when they hit me they made me angry, and even though I was scared, I said, "Go and get it, damnit. Get your gun, then." He didn't move. Finally he said very quietly, "You know I won't." He looked too frightened to move, perhaps because of what he'd heard himself say. "But you can't have him," he said.

He didn't threaten me again. The next threat I heard was from May—through my father. "We'll make Seth hate his mother," she'd said.

Seth

There wasn't much school left, two weeks maybe. The days were getting even hotter, as hot as it had been during Grandmama's funeral when that heat wave came through. And the wind was blowing all the time it seemed, but that helped. I'd come up from down on the creek, sweat covering my face, and when I'd get to the top of the hill, the wind would hit me and cool me off, blow the sweat off me almost. But there was something that didn't feel right about it, too. The wind isn't supposed to blow like that so late in the spring when it gets hot. Sometimes dust and dirt would swirl up with the wind and the air would turn a dirty brown, almost yellow, and all of a sudden the world wouldn't look like the world. It would look like some strange planet where you can't breathe the air and stay alive.

I didn't see Bobby very much after school for a while. His daddy always had him out in the garden, or running trotlines on the river. Johnny too. Mostly I stayed around the store or down in the pasture. Daddy looked worried. He'd all the time have an expression on his face like somebody just died. I almost forgot how he really looked. It was like his real face was hidden. I'd see him watching me around the store and at home, and I'd wonder if I was making him worry, if maybe I was acting different somehow. He'd make me worry about myself when I saw him watching me, like I was dying or something. I tried to stay away from him some of the time. He kept telling me more about Mama, things he hadn't said before, things I still didn't want to hear about or think about. I was by myself a lot, down in the pasture, riding my bike around the Loop Road, walking around the barns with my pellet gun.

One day at school, Bobby asked me to come home with him. He said his daddy had told him he didn't have to work that afternoon, and he said he had a plan for us.

We ended up out in the sedge field behind his house with some kites his mama had bought for us in Demarville. It was a clear day, not as hot as it had been. Johnny was with us too, and later on Frances came out. When she caught up with us, I told her that her hair was the same color as the sedge. She smiled at me and I thought she looked beautiful.

The wind was blowing hard, and it kept the tops of the sedge bent toward the house. The whole field looked like the water out on the Gulf the way it moved in waves with the gusts of wind. And it was so deep and thick in places that it was almost like wading through water. As we walked, I kept thinking how I wanted to dive into it and disappear and not come up for air.

We got our kites up after a few tries. Mine was bright green with a long tail made out of pieces of a ripped sheet. Frances said she had made the tails the night before, had stayed up late doing it. After I let all the string out, I had to fight hard against the pull of the wind. It kept wanting to take the kite from me and send it way up above the clouds, but I played it just right. I'd bring it in a little, then let it back out.

As we stood out there in the tall sedge with our kites high in the air, I thought, This looks just like some kind of picture you might see on a calendar maybe, or a postcard. A bunch of kids or a whole family playing out in some beautiful park on a perfect day. I suddenly felt what those people must feel. After that I didn't think about anything at all except how my kite looked against the blue sky.

Later on, Bobby's mama came out. She had a Green Devil in her hand again, and she was smiling like somebody had just told her a joke, one she probably shouldn't repeat to children but probably would if you asked her to. "I want to fly me a kite," she said around the cigarette in her mouth. We all had to talk loud because of the wind, but she was talking louder than she had to and didn't know it.

"You're not going to fly mine," Frances said. "You can forget that. Not after I made all these tails. Why don't you fly Johnny's? He said he was wishing you'd come out here." She grinned.

"No, I didn't," Johnny said.

"Come on, Johnny. Let your mama fly your kite a minute." She walked over to him, picking her way through the sedge like she was following dance steps. She leaned down over him once she got there and tried to whisper, but didn't do a very good job of it. "Come on now, be good to your mama."

Johnny jerked his hands away from her, and she reached for the ball of string with her free hand. They kept at that for a minute or two, his mama laughing the whole time. Then finally they messed up and the kite flew off. We all watched it for a second and didn't say anything. Then their mama said, "Look at that thing. Why it's up there as—well, as high as a damn kite!" She thought that was pretty funny.

Johnny walked off toward the house and disappeared into the sedge.

"You shouldn't have done that, Mama," Bobby said.

She turned back toward us. The cigarette wasn't in her mouth anymore and she'd dropped the Green Devil. "I know," she said. "I'll go see what I can do to make up for it." She picked up the empty Green Devil, held the bottle upside down in her hand, and started walking back toward the house.

I don't know why I remember all that. Maybe because I

couldn't picture my own mother ever walking out into a field like that, laughing and wanting to fly a kite, or my father, either. He would have come out there, but it would have been different somehow.

Bobby and Frances drove me home later in their old blue truck. Daddy had gotten in from work, and he was mad. I hadn't let anybody know I was going anywhere. He didn't say much, not then. He just stood there in the kitchen by the counter and gave me that look he's got.

After we ate the supper Grandmama fixed that night, Daddy came into my room and sat down in the chair beside the dresser. I knew he would. He'd been coming in a lot lately to talk about Mama. When I saw him come in, I wanted to leave, but there was no way. He started right in about how I hadn't called earlier.

"I've got to know where you are," he said. "You can't just go off places. If something happened to you I wouldn't be able to do anything."

"Yes, sir," I said. "But Bobby's mother was there." I didn't tell him about what she'd been drinking.

"That's not the point," he said. "The point is that I didn't know where you were or who you were with." He looked directly at me and paused a minute. "I don't want to ever lose you," he said. It came out of nowhere, but he was always saying things like that, especially lately.

He went on about how he was trying to be a good father, like Granddaddy had been to him. Then he got to Mama. But this time was different. His voice sounded a way that I can't describe. He wasn't angry at me or anything. He was angry at Mama. But there was more to it than that. It was like if he could talk long enough and hard enough, whatever things he was worried about would go away, disappear. He would be able to stop worrying. His face would go back to looking the way it was supposed to.

"I've told you your mother tried to kill herself—more than once," he said.

"Yes, sir."

"I don't like to tell you these things. But you have to know. The thing I have to make you understand is what her suicide attempts meant. They meant that she was willing to leave you, to desert you, that she didn't care enough about you. Do you understand? She didn't care enough."

"Yes, sir."

"She's told people that she's afraid of me, that she used to be afraid that I would hurt her. You know that nothing could be further from the truth, don't you? I'm the one who saved her and kept her alive. You know I would never hurt her? Please know that. You must know that."

"Yes, sir," I said, and it made me mad that she would say something like that about Daddy. She didn't love him anymore, but I knew he still loved her.

"She's telling lies like this. I don't know why. To hurt me, I guess. But they're lies."

"Yes, sir."

"She's going to take me to court. She wants to take you from me. That's what she wants. She'd said that she wouldn't do this, but she's gone back on her word. Do you understand? She doesn't want us together. She's trying hard to make that happen because she has always resented how close we are. Is that the kind of mother a boy should have?"

"No, sir."

"I don't say these things to keep you from seeing her, if you want to see her, that is. Do you? I want what you want. Tell me. What do you say? Do you want to see her?"

"No, sir. I won't see her," I said. The words just came out, like somebody else said them. They didn't seem like my words.

"Well, all right then," my father said, and for a moment he didn't look so worried in his face.

That night I lay awake in bed for several hours and started to remember something that I hadn't thought about in a long time.

I'd been coming out of my old room one morning, and when I went by Mama and Daddy's door in the hall, I heard Daddy's voice. It seemed like it came right under the crack at the bottom of the door. "I won't let you. I'll have my son with me," he said. I stopped and listened close, but couldn't hear what they said next.

Then I heard Mama. "Go and get it, damnit. Get your gun, then." Her voice was just as loud as his had been, and I stood stock still there in the hall.

"You know I won't," Daddy had finally said, but his voice was quiet this time. It sounded like somebody would sound if they'd just found out about a death, like they didn't have much breath to talk with. But I heard it just the same.

In a minute the door opened. I turned away quick and walked on up the hall, trying to pretend I hadn't been close enough to hear anything, that my heart wasn't pounding. But I stopped all of a sudden and turned around. I couldn't help it, seemed like. Daddy stood by their door. His face was all serious looking, but not scary—not really. He just stood there like he was lost, like he couldn't remember where the hall led to. I heard a drawer slam then in the bedroom and Daddy seemed to come to. He pulled the door shut. I turned and walked up the hall, and Daddy followed me. He never did say anything, and I went in the kitchen.

The next night Daddy came into my room again. He didn't talk long though, not this time. He wanted me to write Mama and tell her how much I wanted to stay where I was, and for her to please not try to make me come live with her, that that wasn't what I wanted. He said not to tell her yet that I didn't want to see her again.

All of this sounded so strange. I hadn't ever thought about having to *tell* her I didn't want to see her. They had just been words I'd said to Daddy the night before. I couldn't imagine writing them to her.

The next day after school, I went to my room and got the kite

I'd brought home from Bobby's. There was a good wind outside, and I didn't want to stay in the house. I wanted to be away from everybody. Daddy was at work, but Grandmama was home. When I walked past her in the kitchen, she looked at the kite in my hand and asked me where I was going. She didn't sound like herself. I told her I was going out in the pasture, that there was a good breeze. "Oh," she said, "I see." Then she turned back toward the sink where she'd been washing dishes.

I walked into the pasture, let some string out, and took a few running steps and tried to get my kite up. It would fly a little ways, then a hard gust would come and crash it into the ground. I wanted to get it way up in the air the way I'd been able to down at Bobby's, wanted to look up and see it against the sky—and that day the sky was just as blue and clear as it had been at Bobby's. It looked like some kind of perfect ocean. I wanted my kite to sail high up into it, wanted to look at that diamond shape and see the long tail trailing behind and not have to think about anything else.

Grandmama came to the pasture gate. I was holding the kite by the cross sticks, about ready to take another running start. I took two steps, stopped, and waited. It took her a while to get to where I stood. She walked slow and was careful to step around the fire ant hills and the cow manure. The wind blew her hair beneath the clear plastic hood she'd put on, and the way she held her head down it was like the wind hurt her face. Her expression made it look that way too. Her mouth was drawn tight and her eyes were squinted.

She finally got to me. "Your Daddy told me that you were going to write your mother a letter," she said. "Don't you think you ought to come in and do it?"

"Yes, ma'am," I said. "I guess so." I knew then that I'd been waiting on her to come out and get me.

Laura

Isurprised them all. I knew that I had to do something to let my son know how much I wanted him, and that I *wasn't* crazy, no matter what he'd been told. I drove to Valhia and called from my father's house, demanding to see Seth. Conrad couldn't say no. Not this close to the court date. I outmaneuvered them. Or so I thought.

When I picked him up Saturday morning in Riverfield, he stood in the driveway with his suitcase beside him. He somehow looked like a stranger waiting on a bus to come through, and the first glance that I got of his face made me doubt the wisdom of what I was doing. His expression looked like that of someone who'd been on the road for days, alone, with little hope of getting home again. He kept turning his head from my car to the door behind him. Then he put his suitcase in the backseat and got in beside me.

"How are you?" I asked.

"Fine," he said, but he wouldn't look at me. The way he sat so stiff, with his hands balled into tight fists, made me feel that he was afraid of talking to me. It was as if he felt that being with me was a betrayal, and I knew then how far his father and grandparents had finally gotten through to him.

"What have you been doing with your summer?" I said. We pulled out of the drive then, just after a big truck had passed.

"Not too much, I guess."

"You must be doing something."

"I go down in the pasture. Ride my bike." His voice sounded tight, as if he had to force the words out.

"What about friends?"

"I see Bobby some."

"Who's he, again?"

"Just a friend. I told you about him once."

All the way to Valhia, our conversation, or what little there was of it, seemed more like an interrogation than simple talk between a mother and son. All I could do was keep my eyes on the road and drive.

We got to Valhia and he put his things away. I'd told him we wouldn't go to Montgomery, and he'd seemed relieved to hear that. He finally came into the living room where his grandfather and I sat on the sofa near the hearth. His hands were in his pockets and he kept looking out one of the windows.

"Do you want a little something to eat?" I said. "I'll fix lunch later, but you can have something now."

"I think I just want to go outside. I'm not really hungry." He still hardly looked at me, or at his grandfather.

"All right," I said, and he walked out of the door.

"It's best to let him go," my father said then. "Let him do what he wants." He was right, I knew, but it sounded strange to hear him, of all people, say such a thing.

He did come in for lunch when I called, but he stayed out of my sight most of the day. I kept watch through the large windows downstairs, and I'd only occasionally see him emerge from out of the trees at the bottom of the hill. Then he'd disappear again, not like a child playing, but like the ghost of a child not wanting to show itself beyond the thick, dark pines.

We ate a big supper that evening, and afterward his grandfather left us alone, intentionally, I'm sure. We went to the living room again and he wanted to watch television.

"The shows I like are on," he said, as if he couldn't be expected to miss them.

I let him watch, but of course I wanted to talk to him, to find the words that would bring my child back to me from out of whatever place he was hiding. Neither of us spoke, though, not even during commercials. Then it began to get dark, and the television screen seemed like nothing more than some dim flickering light whose only purpose was to create shadows for us to hide within.

Another commercial came on, but before I could say anything, he suddenly got up from the sofa. Something seemed very wrong. "Are you all right?" I said. It took him a moment to answer.

"I feel sick," he said.

He walked slowly, clumsily, and before he made it across the room, he went down onto his knees and I heard him retch. I went to him, my only thought that my child needed me, and I knelt beside him on that hard stone floor. But when I put my hand on his back to comfort him, he pulled away like some new reflex had been born in him. Then I felt sick inside.

"Do you think it was something you ate?" I said. It was all I could manage to say.

"No," he said. "It wasn't anything I ate." I guess that was all that needed to be said then. There was no point in us trying to talk further.

During the night I kept checking on him. I'd given him some medicine and he appeared to be sleeping. I hoped he was. It didn't matter that I couldn't.

I took him back the next morning. He asked me if he could go home early. I could hear the apprehension in his voice when he spoke. Let him go, I thought.

The drive over was very quiet, and it seemed to take so little time. Before he got out of the car I told him that I loved him. He looked at me and nodded. At least it was something. Then I watched him walk up the back steps with his suitcase and saw the door open before he got to it. I wondered who stood just beyond it. His father? His grandmother?

On the way home to Montgomery I tried to decide what would be best for my son. I had no answer, not one that I wanted to acknowledge, at least.

Then Seth's letter came on Monday. There was another one later, full of even more hurt, which hardly seemed possible until I read its final lines, but it was the first letter that made me sure that I had to stop fighting. He begged me to let him stay with his father, to please not make him come live in Montgomery. That was his word for me. *Montgomery*. I felt as if I'd been reduced in his heart from someone he loved and who he knew loved him to even less than a place—to nothing but a point on a map. *Don't make me come live in Montgomery.*

And then I thought, they did defeat me after all. They were able to turn love and loss and bewilderment into something that approached fear, something that was close enough for their purposes. And maybe they *would* end up making him hate me, but I hoped there was enough love left in him to keep that from happening.

The second letter came weeks later, not too long after all the papers were final and the visiting times established. I came home for lunch, checked the mail, and found that they had defeated me more soundly than I had known. What they did amounted to violence.

It was a short letter. He told me he was happy, that he was getting used to all the changes, and he thanked me for letting him stay with his father. Then came the final lines. He told me that he'd left a number of his games in his closet. "Please send them to me," he said, "because I won't be coming to Montgomery again."

84

Montgomery, he said. I was reduced again, this time not just into less than a place, less than a point on a map. I was reduced to nothing. I did not exist. I was like my own mother, dead, and my dying had begun, I realized, the day of my mother's funeral, when I first felt that I might really lose him, and now it was over. I'd lost my other child too, lost him, in a way, to *his* father, to the ways of destruction that men so often pass down to each other. It was as if we were all dead things, that my mother's funeral had been a funeral for us all. My only hope was time, and that's what I clung to.

January–April 1975

Seth

The drive up to Ripley, Mississippi, was a long one, but Daddy and I left early in the morning, while it was still dark. We crossed the Mississippi line at Columbus, and by then it wasn't quite as dark. You could see, but everything looked covered in shadows, like in a dream, maybe one you don't want to remember. Going through North Mississippi took the longest. The countryside up there was a little more hilly, and the pine trees looked too small. Their needles didn't grow long enough. It was like they'd been sprayed with something that had stunted their growth.

Daddy had mentioned the trip the first of the week. I'd heard in his voice how much he wanted to go. He said that since we hadn't done anything together—just the two of us—in a long time, that we ought to take a short trip on the weekend. He said he'd been wanting to go up to Ripley because that was where Rafe Anderson, my great-great-grandfather, had once fought in a skirmish along with the Second Alabama cavalry during the War, and that there was supposed to be a historical marker posted. He'd just read about the fight and wanted to see if he could tell by the lay of the land where things had happened.

I didn't really want to go. The truth is that we hadn't been doing much together because whatever he came up with, I didn't want to do. I don't know why. But the week he asked about Ripley, I finally said yes. I'd been bored so much, for one thing. The weather had been bad, cold and wet, and I couldn't get out. I'd just barely started to make friends with a few other boys over the summer—I'd see them at different fishing holes, around the store, at church—but they weren't coming around to the house. Bobby was still my only real friend, and I hadn't seen him much that winter outside of school.

So the trip sounded good, and I like it when Daddy talks about history and about our family. I always listen to his stories, and Grandmama and Granddaddy's, about how my great-great-granddaddy ran away from home and how he fought in the War and how my great-granddaddy challenged a man to a duel. It's almost like they're telling me things about myself. One thing I remember when we used to take trips, with Mama I mean, and Michael too, when he'd still go with us, was that Mama would never let Daddy talk about things he was interested in, old stories and things. She'd make fun of him. It hurt me when she did that, and it hurt Daddy. I thought about that some while we rode along through those scrubby pine trees and hills.

We found the place outside of Ripley about the middle of that morning. There were signs on the highway first: "Historical Marker 1000 Feet," "Historical Marker 500 Feet." Mama used to say the South is so littered with historical markers that they're a driving hazard.

There was a picnic table beside the sign and trash lay all over the ground: bottles, beer cans, paper bags. We got out of the car, and the first thing I did was put on my gloves and button my coat. It was cold, but the sun had come out before we passed through Tupelo and the day was at least pretty.

The marker gave the date June 25, 1863, but it didn't say where the fight took place, just "in this area." Daddy looked around for a while and finally said for us to walk toward the line of woods down to our right. There was nothing but open fields between us and the trees, where it looked like hay probably grew in the spring, but right then the fields were all brown and dead. When we got to the edge of the woods we saw that a barbed-wire fence ran along beside them, and it looked almost like it held the woods in, kept them from spreading out into the field where we stood.

"It's kind of low and swampy in there," Daddy said, "but if I'm right there's an old road back a little way maybe and some high ground. They fought near a swamp." He looked around for a minute. "We're not supposed to trespass. Maybe this one time it will be all right, though," he said and looked at me. "What do you think?"

It surprised me that he was willing to do it. "I think it'll be all right," I said, then smiled. "I want to see where it happened."

He held the brittle, rusted wire apart and I swung my leg over the bottom two strands. When Daddy crossed through and I held the wire for him, I felt like we were both in on something to-gether. We were trespassing, like he'd said, breaking the law. If we got caught, we'd both be in trouble. I could tell that he felt it too because when he stood up straight, out of the wire, he smiled at me in a way I wasn't used to. We watched our breath rise like smoke in the air, and he put his hand on my shoulder.

The woods were thick for a while and the ground was muddy and pools of black water stood all over. Things were even more dark and swampy to the left of us. After a while the woods thinned out and the ground rose. We found something that looked like a dry ditch, and Daddy said it was the old road he was looking for. We followed it and came out of the woods and up onto an open place where small hills stood.

"I think this is the spot," he said. "I can't be sure, but I've got a hunch. There are supposed to be three hills."

He counted them, then started pointing to where things had happened, or to where he thought they'd happened, and told me how the Union troops had come up that road we'd been on and how the Second Alabama had been riding over the crest of the first hill. They'd surprised each other, he said, but didn't waste time trying to back away and form ranks. They pulled out their swords and their sidearms and charged, met halfway down the hill, firing and slashing and yelling. "Imagine the heat on that June day," he said, "and how the smoke from their sidearms rose thick all around them." I watched our breath in the air again and imagined it as smoke.

Daddy's voice made him sound like he was remembering everything he described, and his memory seemed to come back stronger and stronger the more he talked. I could begin to see it all, too. I imagined Rafe Anderson riding a big black horse, holding the reins in one hand, shooting his pistol with the other. And I could see the fight as it spread out across the sides of the hills, see the blue and butternut uniforms of the men and their hats and their long beards. I could hear them shouting. It wasn't like studying history in school, it was like some movie, only it was more real than that. I was there, walking up the middle hill, smelling the smoke and feeling how hot it was, even though it was January and I had my coat buttoned and this was nothing but a field right outside of some small town in Mississippi, just like any other little town in Mississippi or Alabama. For a little while though it seemed more real than the worst thing that had ever happened to me, and it all came through the sound of Daddy's voice.

Then Daddy said, "And there were twenty killed," and his voice stopped. For another minute or so I could still feel and see everything, but then it was gone. There was just me and Daddy.

Twenty people, I thought. I wondered if any of the soldiers had been buried nearby, or if their bones had been scattered and hidden by animals. I imagined what those bones would look like now, how white and broken up. Part of me wanted to find them. They were a secret, and suddenly everything I knew and thought and felt seemed like a secret too. Then I looked at Daddy standing up the hill from me. He looked lonely, and I thought the word *secret* again, almost heard it in the quiet between us, and I thought, What is our secret? What is it that we keep from each other? What is it that we don't say? And I thought, *Mama*. We don't talk about her anymore. To anyone. Neither of us. She is a buried secret.

Standing in the cold, everything felt a little strange, confused, run altogether—bones and quiet and secrets and things you remember without trying to or wanting to.

The two of us walked on around the hills and the edge of the woods. The wind blew in gusts and made us even more cold so that my gloves weren't much help anymore. We finally headed back down the road that looked like a ditch and then crossed through the wire. We each helped the other one through again, and it felt somehow like we were crossing back out of our memories.

We ate at a diner in Ripley. The food wasn't bad. I had country fried steak, and the waitress kept calling me "honey." It made me feel strange. It wasn't like she was my mother or anything.

"What do you think?" Daddy said. "Did we find the right place?"

"Yes, sir," I said. "It felt right."

"Has it been a good trip?"

I nodded my head and didn't say much more. When you know a secret and that secret's on your mind, it keeps you from talking. You're scared you'll bring it up by accident. And then what would you do? How would you talk about it?

We drove out of North Mississippi, and when we finally crossed the Alabama line, it started to get dark, the way it does early in the winter. We crossed the Tennahpush River and Daddy said, "We're not far now. It'll be good to get home."

But Riverfield still wasn't home to me, not yet, even after a year. I felt broken up and scattered, like old bones. I needed a place where I didn't feel I was in pieces, and it seemed like the closest I could come was when I stood in an old place, on old ground, or maybe sat listening to the stories that Daddy or Grandmama or Granddaddy told. Their stories were a place, too, a place in time, and maybe a place to hide.

Conrad

I know what his mother would have said of our trip, that it was a waste, that I tried to spend too much time with him. Then she would have used the chance to have gone on and said that I was hurting him somehow by trying to spend so much time with him, that I always tried to smother him. She always tried to make my relationship with Seth sound unhealthy. She would even tell me that I held him too much when he was a baby. But he was sick, not completely developed. Of course I held him. He needed comfort. She held him too, and she worried like I did. After he was a little older, not sick anymore, I would get home at night after work and play with him in his room while Laura cooked supper. Sometimes I'd pick him up and carry him into the kitchen. It would be warm in there, the smell of food filling the air, and I would think, This is a home we've made, together, the two of us. It's in the very air I'm breathing.

But she would so often tell me I was in her way and want me to leave. I'd take Seth back into his room and play with him, or I'd take him into the living room and sit down on the sofa with him in my lap. Michael would be in there sometimes, but often he'd be playing outside in the neighborhood with boys his age. I would hear them yell and call to each other from up and down the street. When it got too dark, I'd open the door and tell him to come in—if he was nearby, and if he wasn't I'd take Seth in my arms and go out looking for him. The one regret I have during that time is that I perhaps did not spend as much of my time with Michael as he needed.

When Seth got older, I'd take him for walks on warm spring days. We would walk in Oak Park or just around the neighborhood. Sometimes the two of us would come up to Riverfield for the weekend, and I'd take him down in the pasture and show him where I played as a child and tell him about people I remembered. I'd always try to get Laura to go wherever we went, but she usually wouldn't. She'd just tell me how I was smothering Seth, how I would never let him play by himself, how I was with him every minute I was home. I can be overprotective. You worry about your child. If you think he's in danger or threatened in some way, you do anything you think you have to, and I do mean anything. But Laura always exaggerated. I don't know exactly why she chose to look at my relationship with Seth the way she did, but I have an idea.

Her father is a difficult man, and he was demanding on her. He expected perfection in school, with her music lessons, with the work she did for him at his office. I have seen her in tears after the briefest of phone calls from him. "Whenever I see him or talk to him," she would say, crying, "it's as if I become a child again, full of resentment, ready to fight him." She would talk about how difficult he was, how demanding, controlling, smothering, and she got the notion somehow that I would become this same kind of father, I suppose. She saw me show my son attention and could not trust it, could not take it for what it was—love, pure simple love. She had no frame of reference. To her, a father's attention meant only one thing, control.

May

We went to church that Sunday after Seth and his Daddy took their little trip, just like we always do, but we were late. Actually, I wasn't late, I was *made* late. Conrad, Sr., is always slow. Seth looked nice in his gray suit, but it was beginning to fit him too snug in the shoulders. We'd bought it for him right before his grandmother's funeral, his first suit, and we'd bought it a little too big so it would last. But he'd grown a lot since the funeral, and that Sunday I saw just how much.

He didn't like to go to church. He always stared out the window during the sermon, and he never said very much when I asked him afterward what he thought of the preacher's words. He never wanted to go to Sunday school either. "All the other boys go," I'd say. "I'll just go to church with y'all," he'd tell me.

The preacher took the story of Jacob and Esau as his text that morning. Said he wanted to speak on brotherhood and forgiveness. He reminded us of how Jacob forced Esau to sell him his birthright for food to keep from fainting and dying, and how he later disguised himself as Esau and received his father Isaac's blessing of plenty. It was a fine sermon, one of his best. Seth even listened too, I think.

Now that I think about it, it was funny that the preacher talked about brothers, considering who we saw after church when we went out to lunch in Demarville, which is something we hardly ever do.

We ate at the old hotel downtown. They have a big buffet every Sunday and a crowd to match. The food is always good. We got there late, of course. So there was hardly a parking place to be found in front of the hotel, but Son found one beside a flatbed truck. In the lobby the old black ceiling fans spun and put out a cool breeze. There was a long line by this time and the dining room was mostly full. Silverware rattled against plates and people were talking quietly. We stood in the serving line for some time and finally got our food, sat down, and started eating.

"There are Mr. Tyner and Michael," Conrad, Sr., said, like an announcement.

We all stopped eating for a minute in surprise. The two of them sat over in a far corner, beyond a white column. Seth stared down at his plate. Uncomfortable situations have to be met, though. You can't ignore them. At least one of us had to go over and say hello. Neither Son or I could go because of what had happened the last time each of us had seen Mr. Tyner. And I knew Conrad, Sr., wouldn't want to.

"Seth," I said, "you need to go over and speak to them." I knew it would be hard for him, but I felt that we shouldn't all just sit there. Seth looked up at me, and his eyes got big and wide with fear.

"You don't have to go, Seth," his father said. "It'll be all right."

I wanted to say "no," that he did have to go, but didn't. "He ought to at least go over and speak to his brother," was all I said, but in a tone that let Seth know what I meant.

"Whatever you want to do," his father said.

Seth looked toward me again, then put his fork down and got up slowly from the table. "What do I say?"

"Just tell them hello," I said.

I couldn't tell if Mr. Tyner or Michael had seen us, but suspected that they had and were going to pretend they hadn't. When Seth got halfway to their table, near the door to the lobby, he did something beyond my belief. He walked out, just disappeared. Maybe it was because of my poor disposition in general that day, but I got suddenly right aggravated with him and stood up from the table before anybody had a chance to say anything and went after him. He was already out the lobby and halfway up the street toward the drugstore on the corner before I could call to him and make him stop.

I caught up with him and took him by the arm. "That's not the way to behave. Do you understand? You've got to face up to things. That's your brother and your grandfather in there, and you must speak to them."

"Yes, ma'am," he said.

His daddy was outside by that time. He told me later not to get in the way of how he took care of his own child, which is what I would have said too.

Seth went back inside and walked over to Mr. Tyner's table and shook hands with his brother, then Mr. Tyner. He never did sit down, but they did talk for a few minutes, though. When he came back to our table, he didn't say much. In fact, none of us said very much.

Michael

I saw my brother first, then saw the rest of them. I figured they'd already seen us, but didn't say anything at all to Granddaddy, decided I'd just wait to see what would happen. They looked our way a few times, careful-like, and after a while, here came Seth.

When he got near the door to the lobby and turned toward it and walked out, I had to smile. He's my brother after all, I thought. He did what I would have done—got the hell out of there.

His grandmama went to get him, and Conrad got up and followed them. After a few minutes, I leaned across the table to Granddaddy. "Here comes Seth," I said. He looked surprised, but just for a second because there Seth was. He looked bigger and his hair had grown longer, but that wasn't the only difference. It took me a while to see what else there was. His face had changed in some way that I couldn't describe.

"You started shaving yet?" I said and shook his hand.

He didn't know what to say to that but finally mumbled "no." He was real uncomfortable.

"Anything wrong? You feeling all right, little brother?"

"I'm fine," he said.

"How is school?" Granddaddy asked him. "Are you making good grades, Seth?"

"Yes, sir. I'm making mostly A's and B's."

"Grades are important. Always try to make A's. Your mother made A's."

"You got a girlfriend?" I said.

"No."

"Why not? You like girls, don't you?"

"Yes, I like them," he said.

"Then why don't you have a girlfriend?"

"I just don't." He was more nervous now.

"Don't pick at your brother," Granddaddy said. Then, "How are your father and your grandparents?"

"They're doing fine."

"Tell them hello for us. And any time you'd like to come see me, just let me know."

"Yes, sir."

He looked back at me then like he wanted to say something but he wasn't sure what. "Are you still in Florida?" he finally said.

"Well, right now I'm sitting here talking to you, but let's just say I'm on vacation from Florida. I'll be going back, though. You can count on that."

He stood there for a minute with his hands stuck in his pockets.

"You don't want to let your food get cold, do you?" I said.

"No, I guess not."

He walked on back to his table then.

Granddaddy stared at me for a minute after Seth walked away. He didn't seem very happy.

"I'll have to tell your mother we saw him," he said, "and that he looks good. I'll have to tell her where you are too, I suppose."

"Yes, sir," I said. "I guess you will."

We went back to eating then, without saying much.

What I'd told Seth was true. I did plan on going back to Florida, but I'd lost my job on the tug. You could say that the tug master and I'd had a personality conflict. So I'd left Florida early

101

in the week and showed up at Granddaddy's door about ten o'clock the night before. For some reason he hadn't seemed surprised to see me, just glad, which is more than what I'd probably have been able to say about my own mother.

I didn't plan on staying in Valhia too long. Enough time to regroup, maybe earn a little money. I could already hear that ocean calling me from all those miles away. I love the way a tug cuts right through the choppy blue while it laps and pulls at you, the way the sun reflects off the water and hits your eyes. And at night when you're sitting out on the beach with a pint of something in your hand, the waves call out of the dark like some voice that you can't quite understand. It makes you think about things, about what's happened to you or been done to you.

So I wanted to get back. But I did stay awhile, and as it turned out, a hell of a lot longer than I should have. Just like my brother once took something that belonged to me, I took something from him, and Conrad, too.

Seth

The school bus passed Granddaddy's store where I always got off, but I'd told Miss Williams, the woman who drives the bus and gives music lessons at school, to keep going. She'd looked at me funny in the rearview mirror, like I must have been wanting to do something wrong. We crossed the highway and onto the Loop Road, and she ground through the gears. Then we passed Jackson Quarter, and I wondered what it was like to live there in that poor section. When we got to the place where the bus follows the Loop on around to the left, I got off and took the little road to the right that leads to Bobby's house. It's about a mile walk, full of pot holes and cracks. They don't ride the bus. Their mama takes them to school or Frances drives.

Bobby and his brother Johnny stood out in the yard when I walked up. Bobby was wearing a big coat that looked like it was probably his daddy's, but it wasn't all that cold out. I'd left my jacket at school.

"Where'd you come from?" Bobby said.

"I rode the school bus and walked the rest of the way. What have y'all been doing?" I said, then heard hollering from inside just as Frances came walking out. Their mama and daddy were arguing in the kitchen, standing across the table from each other.

"You son of a bitch," their mama hollered.

Frances closed the door and came on out into the yard, but we could still hear a little bit when they'd get real loud. We all stood around for a few minutes. Then Bobby climbed up in the back of their blue truck, and we followed him and sat and watched through the windows. We could see pretty good because we were up high. Neither Bobby or his brother seemed like they were embarrassed, at least not much. It was like, "Well, Seth's here, he can watch just like we always do." I don't know what Frances was thinking.

Their mama kept reaching toward the table and then throwing *something*. She'd reach, then throw. Reach, throw.

"She got into that bag of potatoes," Frances said.

They kept right on hollering at each other, and sometimes we could make out words like "goddamnit" and "bitch."

"Frances, what are they fighting about?" Bobby said.

"Daddy spent a bunch of money on a truck, only now the truck won't run and this is the first she's heard of any of it."

"Where's the truck?"

"Broken down on the other side of Demarville."

"What's Daddy gon' do?" Johnny said.

"Fix it and sell it, I hope, if Mama doesn't kill him first."

Their mother stopped throwing potatoes then and ran around the table toward their daddy. Then they both disappeared down the hall. Things were quiet in the house for a minute, but they didn't stay that way. The two of them came charging back into the kitchen. This time it was mostly their daddy yelling, even though we couldn't make out much of what he was saying.

"He's going to give it back to her," Frances said.

But then we heard a loud "goddamnit" from their mama and she really cut loose. I was thinking, How long can this go on?

While we sat there and listened from the back of the truck, I finally stopped hearing what was going on inside and remembered what their mama had said about me when Mighty Man had been there. "He ain't never seen nobody like us."

Frances suddenly jumped off the back of the truck. "I've had enough of this," she said and marched toward the house. Neither Bobby or Johnny looked surprised.

"She does this sometime," Bobby said.

By then she had the door opened and stood at the top of the steps. "Both of you shut up!" she said. "We can hear you outside. Besides, we got company. So shut up."

She went on in and closed the door behind her after that. We all stayed in the truck and waited to see what would happen. I couldn't believe what she'd done, how she'd stood there and talked to her parents. I tried to imagine talking that way to my father, and then to my grandmother, tried to picture standing in front of each of them and raising my voice like that, but I couldn't do it. Frances had done it, though.

"If they ain't thrown her out of the house by now," Bobby said, "they'll shut up."

We waited some more, and sure enough, they were quiet. In a little while, Frances came walking back out. Her eyes had a hard stare in them, and I noticed what color they were for the first time—a deep blue, like the ocean. Her blond hair was pulled back and the muscles were stretched tight across her high cheek bones. Her face looked like something on a statue.

"Bobby, Daddy says y'all got to clean out the tool shed. He wants me to take Seth on home."

"Are they done fighting?" Bobby said.

"Hell, I guess so," she said. It was the first time I'd heard her cuss. It made her sound grown, like an adult, like somebody you had to listen to. Her body looked grown too, not like girls in my class, and not even like girls in her class, really. There was something different in her. If you saw her walking with a child, holding its hand, you'd think she was its mother. That's what she looked like.

"I'm glad you came by," Bobby said. "Come on back anytime."

He and Johnny walked on off toward the shed, and I got in the cab of the truck while Frances walked around to the other side. She climbed in and slammed the door hard, cranked the truck, and backed out into the road. "The heater won't work," she said.

She drove to where I'd gotten off the bus, then turned onto the Loop Road. In a little while we passed Jackson Quarter. Neither one of us said anything. When we got to the highway she stopped. "Are you ready to go home?"

"Not really," I said.

"Neither am I," she said and sounded kind of disgusted.

She turned left onto the highway instead of right, then turned down the dirt road in front of the Bait Shop and I knew we were headed toward The Landing. She drove fast and the dust kicked up behind us, in one big, long brown cloud. When we got to the top of the hill that leads down toward the Tennahpush River, she slowed to a crawl. The water was high and even more muddy than usual. Instead of driving to the boat ramp, though, so we could see the water up close, she turned down the road that weaves through the trees and the campsites, which were all empty because of the time of the year. She parked on a high bank above the river. There's a big bend there and the water stretches out wide, and there's even a small deserted island on the far side that I've always wanted to see up close.

"Let's get out," she said, which I did because I felt like I was supposed to mind whatever she said. We sat down at the picnic table and looked at the water below us. It ran fast and was full of whirlpools and floating logs and limbs that would get sucked under and then pop back up way down stream. I'm a good swimmer, but I wondered if I'd be able to keep from drowning if I jumped in.

"Mama and Daddy aren't always like that," she said. She was still looking toward the water. "Just sometimes. It's the way they are. They fight, but they love each other."

"I know," I said. And I did. Their fighting seemed normal, for them. It surprised me that Frances felt like she had to say something about it.

"I get tired of it sometime, though," she said. "They drink too much, too. They'll go months without drinking. Then it'll be every day for a couple of weeks." She was quiet for a second and finally turned toward me. Her blond hair was still pulled back around her ears, and she was sitting so close to me that I could see the small freckles on her neck. She didn't have any make-up on, but there was a red color in her cheeks from the cold and her eyes looked even deeper blue than before. It was like her face was naked, and there was something warm in her eyes. I knew that she would never tell me a lie.

"What about your parents?" she said. "Did they fight?"

"Not like yours," I said.

"Then how?"

"They didn't yell, but you could always feel when they were mad. But it wasn't like they were ever mad about one thing exactly. They were always more than just mad."

"What do you mean?" she said.

"I don't know. I don't know how to tell you."

"Was it always bad?"

"Pretty much."

"Have you seen your mama any?"

"No."

"Do you miss her?"

I didn't say anything to that. Then she asked me if I'd seen my brother, and it surprised me until I remembered that she'd seen him before. It seemed like she really wanted me to answer her, but I didn't, even though I felt like I was disobeying her.

I sat there and stared at a log floating down the river. Then Frances did a strange thing. She took off her blue jean jacket and put it around me, then put one arm around my waist. I felt warm suddenly, and I hadn't even realized I was cold. A barge came past after a while, one so big and so loaded down with coal that the fast-moving water didn't seem to make any difference. It might as well have been as calm as on a summer day, and once the barge pushed its way out of the wide bend, it looked almost too big for the river, like it was going to scrape the bank on both sides and Frances and I would have been able to step out onto it and been carried away.

Conrad

I had pulled down into the Bait Shop parking lot, looking for him, when I saw the two of them in the blue truck, about to turn onto the highway from off of The Landing road. I'd already been looking for an hour or so, and I knew what truck to look for because I'd been down to Bobby's house and found out Seth had been there.

I'd talked to James, Bobby's father, out in the yard. It was the first time I'd seen him in a number of years, and for one brief moment I felt as if the two of us could take our pocketknives, walk out into the woods behind his house, and carve our initials into a tree, a tree in which I would then fully expect him to climb to the very top of where the small branches would barely hold. I smiled at the thought of that and asked him about Lois, his wife. He said she was inside and not feeling well. Then I asked about his brother, who was living, last I'd heard, down in South Alabama. I finally asked, very hesitantly, about Jean, his younger sister, who I had once dated. "She's still married and still living in Mississippi," he said and suddenly seemed as if he wanted to change the subject. I started to ask if she had children, but didn't. There was that awkward moment then when neither of us knew what to say and, luckily, we both had the good sense not to say anything.

I drove on around the rest of the Loop, then finally pulled into the Bait Shop parking lot. When I spotted Seth and Frances I waved them down. She pulled across the highway and parked beside me. I had seen her before, of course, but it had been a long time and I was struck by how much she looked like James's sister. It wasn't as if they looked like twins, but certainly like sisters, that's if it had been twenty years earlier. She smiled from inside the cab and waved. She looked very pretty, and I saw the way Seth looked at her as he handed her the jacket he had just taken off. It was the same way I had once looked at Jean.

Seth got out of the cab, and Frances waved but drove away before I could speak to her. "You've got some explaining to do," I said to Seth.

"Yes, sir."

"You can't just go off and not tell anyone where you are. We've talked about this before, haven't we?"

"Yes, sir."

"What did you think you were doing?" I said.

"I just wanted to go see Bobby. Frances was bringing me home, but she wanted to go look at the river first."

"You'll have to be punished," I said. "You know that, don't you?"

"Yes, sir."

I told him he was grounded for a week. No going anywhere. Not even down into the pasture, I said. I hated to do it.

That evening I went to the store right before closing time. I like to be there then because I'm always a little afraid that someone might try to rob my father when the cash drawer is at its fullest. He'd already let his part-time help go home, and he was there by himself. He said my mother had been there to add up all the charge tickets, but that she'd left a little while ago.

"Is there anything I can do?" I said.

"Not really. I've just got to finish counting the drawer. Did you find Seth?" he said.

110

"Yes, sir."

"He was all right, wasn't he?"

"Yes, sir."

"Sometimes you've got to let a boy do the things he has naturally got to do. That's the way I always did with you."

"I know."

"Where did you find him?" he said.

"I went down to James's looking for him. You know he likes to go there?"

"Uh-huh," he said. He went back to counting money. I knew he didn't approve.

"I don't want to stop him from going."

"I don't reckon so," he said. "But do you think it's a good idea for *you* to go down there?"

"I don't know. Perhaps not."

"So where exactly did you find him?"

"He was with Frances. She was giving him a ride home."

"Uh-huh," he said again.

We both let it drop. There wasn't any need in bringing up something neither one of us wanted to talk about.

Michael

Granddaddy put me to work in his law office indexing land deeds in great big ledgers. I had to have a job, but you want to talk about some bullshit! The southwest corner of the northeast section of township . . . Hour after hour I recorded that stuff. Nothing anybody should be doing.

Sometimes he'd get me to run errands—go to the post office or the bank, look something up in the probate office. At least he gave me credit for having sense. But he'd get mad sometimes, like when he'd send me to mail a letter and I'd be gone an hour. I'd see somebody, some girl maybe, and stop and talk, or go to the lunch counter in the old drugstore, and time would get away from me, slip out of my mind and slide on down the street, you might say. Hell, once or twice it climbed up the goddamn pole to the five o'clock whistle down at the fire station and announced itself.

Late one afternoon I walked down to the gas station to pick up the El Camino Granddaddy let me drive—I'd had to sell my car—and that's when I saw Frances. She'd stepped out of the drugstore, looking fine as wine.

"Hello there, lady," I said. "Remember me?"

She smiled. "You're Seth's brother, Michael." She was wearing a pair of blue jeans and a yellow sweater.

"So what are you doing in the big city?"

112

"Running some errands for Mama," she said and smiled again in a kind of nervous way.

"I'm on an errand too. Got to pick up my grandfather's truck. It needed a little work."

"He's the lawyer with the mansion, isn't he?"

"That'd be him, but it's not exactly a mansion."

"I've heard it's nice, though. You can't really see it through all those woods."

"Well, I tell you what," I said. "You walk down to the station with me, and I'll take you for a little ride and let you see the house."

"I've got stuff to do," she said real quick and looked off down the street like she was waiting on a friend.

I had to say the right thing, I knew, so she wouldn't get away. But it's one of my talents. She was standing there thinking how much she'd like to go, trying to decide how respectable it would be.

"I don't mean go inside," I said. "Just take a minute and drive up that hill so you can see it. Besides, I've got to get back to the office. I'm working for my grandfather right now. And anyway, it's not like I'm some complete stranger."

So she gave in after a respectable protest, and we took us a little pleasure ride. She started talking about Seth. Probably the only thing she could think of. He wasn't exactly what was on my mind at the moment, but I let her talk.

"He comes down to the house a lot to see my brother," she said. "I think he misses his mama."

"Probably so," I said, not really wanting to have to think about our mother.

"Do you see him much? Do you go by and see your daddy?"

"He's not my father."

"He's not?"

"No. We've got the same mother, but different fathers. Mine lives in Selma now. He's from here, though."

"I didn't know," she said.

We were pulling up the driveway by that time, and I had to drop the truck into low gear to make it up the hill. She started saying how pretty it all was, the way the trees grew over the drive, how the wide paths cut through the dogwoods.

"He built it for my grandmother a few years ago," I said. "The house, everything."

"I bet she loved it. Especially since it was all for her."

"She did," I said, and then I thought about Grandmama and wished all of a sudden that Frances wasn't in the truck with me, that it was just me in those woods and that time could slip away and run backwards to when Grandmama was alive. I popped the clutch hard and stepped on the gas, and the truck shot on up the rest of the hill. Frances looked at me strange, like "What was that all about?" but the look on my face must have told her she'd best not ask.

We got out and started walking around the house. She kept saying how nice it was, that she'd never seen a house built of stone, and when she saw the end of the house that faces down the hill and toward the woods, the end that's nothing but two levels of glass, she couldn't believe it.

"Y'all must be rich," she said.

I laughed. "No. Granddaddy's got some money, and he's worked for it, but believe me, he's the only one in the family who's got any real money."

We walked on up the hill then, around the other side of the house, past the terraces and stone walkways. "Wish I lived in a place like this," she said.

"Maybe you do and maybe you don't," I said. "Next time I'll show you inside."

She smiled at that. Don't ask a woman if there will be a next time, just tell her.

We got in the truck and rode on down the hill and back toward town.

"You know," she said when we turned onto the Square, "the other day Seth and I went for a ride together. Now we are."

"Y'all getting close?" I said.

"I don't know. I think maybe he's starting to think of me almost like a mama."

"Is that so?" I said.

"Maybe."

"You want to have kids some day?"

"I guess. Probably."

"So you're getting in a little practice now. Is that it?"

"No. I don't know." She looked at me. "I didn't think about it like that."

"I'm sure you're good for him," I said, easing back a little.

We stopped beside her car and she got out. "Thanks," she said.

"I'll be seeing you." I didn't say when, and didn't ask her out like I knew she must have wanted me to. I'd wait on that. Don't ever let a woman have what she wants *when* she wants it.

I watched her while she walked away. She could feel me watching, and odds are she was smiling. What a fine little mama, I thought.

When I got back to the office, Granddaddy wanted to know what had taken me so long. I told him the truck hadn't been ready, that I'd had to wait. "I'm surprised to hear that," he said.

On Friday he handed me my first paycheck at the end of the day. I took a look at the amount there in his office. I didn't like what I saw. "I thought it would be more," I said.

"It should have been."

"What do you mean?"

"Your pay has been docked."

"Why?" I said.

"Think, Michael. You tell me why."

"I wouldn't know," I said, which was the truth, of course.

"Stop wasting time outside the office. When you work for me, your time doesn't belong to you."

I walked out then and let the door slam shut. I stayed out late that night getting drunk, then got up early the next morning, slipped past my grandfather's room, and went for a little road trip in the old El Camino. It turned into an overnight excursion. Sometimes you never know how long you'll be gone or where you'll end up.

Conrad

I had been reading again on a Sunday morning about the Hornets Nest at Shiloh Chapel, how Confederate troops stormed it twelve times before taking the position. Such horrible and bloody fighting, yet they won so many positions that first day, only to lose, finally. How does one make sense of that? And why did General Johnston have to fall, a man so completely honorable and decent?

I put my book down when the bell rang and walked to the door. Michael stood there with his hands in his pockets, trying to protect himself against the cold. Have you come in peace or to do battle? I wondered as I opened the storm door.

"Is Seth here?" he said. That was all.

"No. Everyone's at church. Why don't you come on into the living room and wait?"

"All right," he said and stepped inside. The smell of cigarette smoke came from his clothes, and there was a hint of alcohol on his breath. He didn't look as if he had bathed since the day before.

In the living room he sat down in a chair across from me and looked about for a moment, not as if he didn't know what to say, but perhaps as if he *had* something to say and didn't know how to begin.

"So what have you been doing?" I said.

"I'm working in the office for Granddaddy."

"Good. Are you going to stay up here long?"

"I don't know," he said.

"You're out fairly early on a Sunday morning, aren't you?"

"Yeah, I guess so. Well actually, I've been to Selma. Kind of an unexpected trip, you might say. I went down yesterday to see somebody."

"Your father?" I said.

"Yeah." He looked surprised, as if I had discovered some secret of his, seen through his mazework of half-truths, lies, and riddles.

"I always liked your father, Michael. We played football together, back when the helmets were still made of leather."

"Oh, yeah?" he said.

"Jack was one of the best athletes I've ever seen. He once took a kickoff at the one-yard line and ran ninety-nine yards for a touchdown. But a penalty was called against us. They kicked off again, and this time Jack took the ball about two yards deep in the end zone and ran for another touchdown. I couldn't believe it, and I'd never been so happy to see anything in my life. I'm the one who had drawn the penalty. After the first run-back, he didn't say a word about the penalty. After the second one he walked over and said, 'Thanks for that last block, wouldn't have made it in without it.'"

Michael just stared at me as I told him the story—no smile, his face like a mask, and not a word at the end. It occurred to me then that I had probably told him a story he didn't know, and that he didn't like hearing about his father from me. Perhaps he felt as if I knew his father better than he did, and resented it.

"So how is your father?"

"Fine," he said and leaned back in his chair and spread his knees a little wider.

We were silent after that, both of us wanting to ask questions—Michael probably wanting to know how I knew his father lived in Selma, I wondering how long he'd been seeing his father, and if Laura knew about it. Laura never spoke much about Jack, but she made it clear that he wasn't a good husband or father.

"My father told me a story about you, too, just yesterday," Michael said then, the tone of his voice implying, as it almost always did, that he knew some secret. You could ask him what time it was and he would either lie to you, make you think he was lying, or tell you in a we'd-better-keep-this-to-ourselves kind of voice.

"What story did he tell, Michael?"

"Just about when y'all were younger," he said.

"So are you going to tell me?"

He shrugged his shoulders and wouldn't look toward me, then began popping his knuckles, an old nervous habit of his.

The back door opened then. My parents and Seth were home from church. Michael rose from his chair, unaware, I'm sure, that he was displaying the manners his mother and I had taught him. If only he had stopped and thought for a moment he would probably have remained seated.

"Looks like we've got company," my mother said as she walked into the living room.

"How you, Michael?" my father said. "Ain't seen you in a long while."

Michael shook both their hands. "Nice to see y'all," he said, again, his manners showing through without his thinking, as if he were unsettled.

He shook Seth's hand very formally, no punch in the arm or hand on his shoulder, which struck me as a bit strange.

"How are things, Seth?" he said.

"Fine," Seth said and looked away from his brother and toward me, as if I could ever explain Michael.

Then Michael just stood there, and I wondered if maybe he hadn't come to see his brother at all, but that left *me*, and why would he come to see only me?

"Will you eat dinner with us? We'd love to have you," my mother said.

For a moment it appeared that he might say yes, but he finally shook his head. "I don't believe so. I'd best go in a few minutes," he said. "I was just passing through on my way from Selma."

"But you must have just gotten here," my mother said. "Won't you stay and eat?" She can't help but want to feed people, it seems. She can take great pleasure in such simple things.

Michael headed toward the back door, walking slowly. It seemed odd that he would leave so soon, as if his reason for coming had suddenly been interrupted.

"Glad you came, Michael. You're welcome anytime," I said, then told Seth to walk him outside. I felt like Seth might have wanted a few minutes with his brother.

After the two of them walked down the back steps and my mother went into the back of the house to change, my father turned to me. "Been drinking," he said in a low voice. "Looks like all night."

"Yes, sir." I said. "Looks that way."

"Smells it, too," he said. "Maybe Seth don't need to be spending a lot of time with him. Might get himself some foolish notions."

"Yes, sir," I said. "You could be right."

May

The squash casserole needed to cook a few more minutes is why dinner was late. Son didn't have much to say at the table. I don't know what he and Michael had been talking about when the three of us walked in, but whatever it was, it must not have been good. Seth didn't have much to say during dinner either, and wouldn't even take the last piece of cornbread when I offered it.

Michael never has spent much time with us. He always stayed with Emily and Mr. Tyner when he'd come up to visit. But that was all right. We understood why.

He was a sweet boy. He always liked to wear a little cowboy outfit that I bought him. He was real cute. Real polite too. And he sure loved his mama. He'd follow her around and if he saw all of a sudden that she wasn't in the room, he'd want to know where she'd gone and start running around looking for her.

Conrad was a good daddy to him. He's always been good at drawing, and on Michael's sixth birthday, not long after Seth was born, they had a little party, and Conrad drew cartoon characters on all the balloons. He gave one to each child, and the best one to Michael. A pirate. He worked on it the longest.

After Michael got to be a teenager, though, we hardly ever saw him, only heard about him getting into trouble, causing problems at home. Such a shame. Both Conrad and Laura did all they could, I guess. Laura even put him in reform school, which was the right thing to do.

After we ate and cleared the table, Son helped me with the dishes, like usual. I asked him what Michael had had to say before we came in. Just a sort of general question, at least that's how I wanted it to sound.

"Only that he's working for his grandfather," he said.

But there had to have been more. He looked too far away in his eyes, like he'd gone to another place, or maybe back to some memory, to something maybe he wished had never happened, and I didn't want to think about what that might be. It's best not to go back to memories too much.

Michael

I'd been just about flying in that old three-on-a-tree El Camino. The engine was wound out in third and I was wound up, half drunk on a Saturday afternoon and a pint of Jack Daniels and headed down an old farm-to-market road to Selma, passing country stores and shacks like they were sitting still, which, of course, they were. But I wasn't, not by a damn sight. I'd bought the pint that morning at the State Store. I would've bought a fifth, but decided to go the less expensive route. In other words, I was cheap, wanting to squeeze every penny out of that piece of paper my grandfather called a paycheck.

Downtown Selma looked like a fire had run through it—it always does—a fire that just got tired finally and quit before it finished the job and actually burned anything all the way down to the ground. And the people there must figure that since the buildings are still standing, that that's good enough and don't ever try to fix anything or clean anything up.

He wasn't in when I got there. Some woman in a dirty tank top and no bra told me she guessed he'd be back after a while. She was the only person in the place. "He don't never tell me where he's going or when he'll be back. You his boy?" she said.

"Yes, ma'am."

She laughed. At what I didn't know. "I ain't ever heard him say he had any kids, but you look exactly like him," she said.

I liked hearing that last part, but she could have left off the first of it.

I got a beer and waited, but didn't have to wait long. He walked in and spotted me through his shades. They were so dark I couldn't see his eyes, and he kept them on when he sat down beside me at the bar. It feels strange not to see somebody's eyes. You can't read what they're thinking. It keeps you from knowing what to say next, throws you off.

"You still in Florida?" he said.

"No. I had to leave."

He just nodded his head at that and didn't ask any questions, like he understood. But hell, you'd think he would have asked.

"I'm staying in Valhia with Granddaddy," I said.

He nodded his head again and motioned to the woman in the tank top. She opened a beer and brought it to him, then went and sat back down at the other end of the bar. He took his sunglasses off and blinked his eyes. "You still got that pistol?" he said.

I wished he'd left his glasses on then. It was almost like he couldn't see me either when they were on. "Yes, sir," I said.

"Good. You didn't sell it or anything, did you?"

"No," I said.

"You working?"

"That's what I wanted to talk about. I've been working for Granddaddy in the office." He laughed a little at that, snorted really. "I hate the work and the pay's not too good. I was wondering if you might could give me a job here?" I let out the breath I'd been holding real slow so he couldn't see.

"You ain't twenty-one yet, are you?"

"No."

"Then I can't do it." He said it like he was maybe glad I wasn't twenty-one yet, but it was hard to tell.

"Nobody would have to know."

"The cops could close me down. I can't take the chance, as much as I'd like to help you out. You understand?"

"Yes, sir." I started to ask him if he knew of any jobs around, one where he might could put in a word for me, maybe something on the river, but I let it go. He probably would have done it all right, but he might have gotten to thinking I'd ask to move in with him next, him and his wife, maybe live in their basement or something for a while. But I wasn't going to ask him that, no way. And if he'd asked me if that's what I'd had in mind, I'd have told him no, that wasn't what I'd had in mind at all, not for one damn second.

"How's Dixie?" I said then, changing the subject. That's his wife, common-law, anyway.

"She's all right. She's gone down to Mobile, where she's from."

"That where you met her?"

"Yeah," he said and took a drink from his beer. "I lived there for a while. Met some fine women there, too. A damn sight better than the ones in Valhia. You stay away from the girls in that town. And for God's sake don't marry one." He laughed.

"I met one from Riverfield," I said. "Named Frances."

"What's her last name?" he said. "I might know her people."

"Sibley."

He looked at me funny. "I knew her mama," he said. "Last I heard she was living in the great state of Mississippi."

"But she lives in Riverfield," I said, thinking something didn't sound right here, that he must have the wrong people in mind.

"No. That ain't her mama. That's James's crazy wife, Lois."

"Then who's her mother?"

"Jean. James's sister."

"This is confusing," I said.

"Jean got pregnant when she was young, and James and Lois was already married and they took the baby in."

"Does Frances know?" I wondered.

125

"Maybe not. You'd be surprised at what people don't know, what doesn't get told."

"Who's her father?"

He took another drink of his beer and cocked his head a little bit sideways, like he was deciding something. "Conrad," he said.

My mouth dropped, but I tried to catch myself and not let on how much it shocked me. You don't want to show too much of what you're thinking. He must have seen the look on my face at first, though.

"It's not like there aren't at least a few people around who know about it," he said. "You don't ever see him anymore, do you, now that he and your mama have split?"

"Every once in a while," I said.

He looked at me sideways again, like he was studying somebody's face in a game of draw poker, trying to decide whether or not to bluff.

"Really it was just a rumor," he said. "Conrad dated her for a while. A lot of other people did too. It could've been anybody. Conrad probably ain't really the father."

A lie can be a good thing, whether you're telling it or somebody else is. Because if somebody else tells one, their lie can tell you what the truth is better than anything, if you know it's a lie. And I can spot a lie and know it for what it is, unless I need to believe the lie, then it becomes the truth and I'll use it. But I'd just heard a lie and it made me know the truth, and the good thing was it was truth I could use.

We kept drinking until late in the afternoon. The woman lined them up for us, one after another. Then my father said, "I got some business to see to. You take care," and he put on his shades and walked out. Didn't say where he was going or what kind of business it was. Didn't invite me along or say come on to the house after a while. Hell, I've never even been to his house. Maybe he did have business. Or maybe he was just tired of talking to me, the only goddamn son he's got, as far as I know.

126

"Don't let it bother you," the woman said. "He does the same thing to me and Dixie. Just walks away. Anything else you want to drink is still on the house. My name's Doris."

I didn't say anything to that, didn't even look toward her. Just drank my beer.

The place started getting crowded about seven o'clock. Somebody punched up some country music on the jukebox and it didn't stop playing. I waited to see if my father would come back, then gave up on him and shot a few games of pool against some boys who said they were from Slapout, Alabama. One of them made a joke about the woman behind the bar. Said those tits of hers were riding pretty low and heavy, but if they were too much of a strain on her she could always just sling them over her shoulders. She'd have to be careful not to sit on them though, he said, but seeing how far her ass hung down, that more than likely wouldn't be a problem.

I got up in the guy's face, holding the pool stick crossways between us. "She's a good lady," I said. "Her name's Doris and she doesn't need some peckerwood like you running her down." I waited on him to shove me so we could all find out just how strong that pool stick was made. You might think it was a stupid thing for me to do, but when you're wanting to fight, when you feel the need, it's like being with a woman. You'll say whatever you've got to say, and you'll say it to whoever you've got to say it to.

"I'm going to do your drunk ass a favor," he said. "I'm in a good mood tonight and so I'm not going to open up a can of whup-ass on you." Then he walked away while I cussed at him.

I danced with some long-legged girl in cowboy boots for a couple of songs. We might have made out some in the truck, or maybe I'm thinking about some other girl on another night.

Conrad

The truth can never be kept completely hidden. And maybe that fact is punishment for the people who attempt to hide it—deserved punishment. Michael's father was one of the people who would have heard the rumors, and there are always rumors.

Jean was much younger, but smart, and although she never said, you could tell that she had plans for herself. She was shy when I first saw her in the store after coming out of the air force, but she had a self-assurance that many people never achieve. Maybe this is what told everyone who knew her that she would leave here, would live a different kind of life from the family she was born into.

She was serious, but she knew how to make me laugh at myself, at my own seriousness. Perhaps she could make me laugh because she *was* younger, still a schoolgirl in some ways. And there I was, headed back to college and toward whatever life awaited me. Perhaps I wanted to stop time, if only for a moment.

But things happen that aren't a part of the plan, even if you're not exactly sure what the plan is.

We reached what one might call an agreement, a kind of settlement, to use the cold language of law, a language that men use so often to obscure their actions, but the agreement this time was not made between men—it was made between a man and a woman, or a girl rather, and the property in question was not a pasture or prime bottom land or a lot on the town square, and the proposal was made by the woman, no matter how young, with her own interest in mind. Yet I can't absolve myself or point blame. I am just as guilty. I entered into collusion, and even now resort to the language of law in trying to explain what is really a matter of the heart.

But the day Jean asked me to drive her down to The Landing, that warm spring day when the river was almost at flood stage, my words did come from the heart. At least that's what I wanted to think then. Where her words came from I don't know, perhaps from her parents, or perhaps from some cold place within her, some place that she had to find.

We parked out on a point of land where the creek that runs through my father's pasture finally enters the river, the Tennahpush. The tables there were wooden then, not cement, and we got out of the car and sat on one of the benches beside an old burned spot on the ground surrounded by small stones.

"I'm going to have the baby," she said and folded her arms beneath her breasts.

"I know. I never asked you not to," I said, surprised. "I wouldn't even know where to go."

"There are places. A doctor I heard about in Tuscaloosa will do it. And there's a black woman in Jackson Quarter."

"Did you really think about doing that?"

"For a while."

"I can't believe it," I said.

"Wouldn't you be relieved? Isn't it what you want? You're just too scared to ask."

"No," I said. "But you're going to have it, aren't you?"

"Yes."

"Then we need to go ahead and get married."

She didn't answer and it was then that I realized my statement was really a question.

"It will be all right," I said. "We'll be good parents. We'll work things out."

She ran a hand through her blond hair and tilted her head downward so that her face was hidden in the crook of her arm. "I'm going away," she said and then looked up at me.

"What do you mean?"

"I've got some cousins on Mama's side who live in Phoenix City. When school's out, I'm going there to have the baby. I can still hide it until then."

"You're going to put it up for adoption? What about us?"

"James and Lois are moving to Prattville, and he's going to work in the paper mill down there. They're going to take the baby and raise it."

"And what about us?" I sat back down on the bench and took her hand. She pulled it away and looked out toward the river at some point I couldn't see.

"I'm going to the women's college in Mississippi, over in Columbus," she said.

"So you don't want to marry me?"

"Do you love me?"

I didn't answer.

"I don't know if I love you, either," she said, and at that moment she looked like a grown woman, much older than me.

"So you've got it all planned out? What about me? Do I get to see the baby? Be its father?"

"No. You don't. And I don't get to be its mother. So don't pretend you're the only injured person here."

"Is there anything I can do?"

"Yes. I want you to promise to never say anything about any of this. Not to anyone. Ever. People will think the baby belongs to Lois. They'll be down in Prattville and won't come home until after time enough for her to have had a baby. The baby will think I'm its aunt."

"At least you'll get to see it."

"There's just one other thing I have to ask."

"What?"

"Will you send money?"

"To you?"

"No. To James and Lois. For the baby. Every month until it's grown."

"Yes," I said.

"And you won't say anything? You won't try to take the baby as yours?"

"No. I won't."

"You promise?"

I felt as tangled and knotted as vines running up a tree in those thick woods around us. I would never get to see my own child, never teach him how to hunt or see her in her first dress. But part of me was relieved, and that was the part of myself I hated the most.

So Jean left. She had Frances and went to college and finally got a job in a bank in Tupelo. Then got married. That was the last I heard, not that any of it came from her. I wrote her twice her first year of college, after I was back in school myself, but never heard from her. Perhaps she knew that I was only trying to assuage my sense of guilt and she didn't want to be reminded of her own; or it may be that she didn't want to use me as I was attempting to use her, understanding on some intuitive level that both of us would end up making excuses and telling each other that we did what we had to do, what was best for all, including Frances. That was one form of collusion she would not enter into.

I did what she asked and sent money each month to James and Lois. It was always a painful day. Probably Jean sent money too, and felt the same sense of pain as she stood in the post office and dropped the envelope that did not contain a letter to our daughter, but merely a check, dropped it down the slot and walked out of the sterile lobby of a federal building.

Frances was a beautiful child. I first saw her in church at Easter when Laura and Michael and I had come up from Montgomery for a visit. Laura and I had been married only about a year at the time. We sat with Michael between us, his legs hanging off the front of the pew, and he kept looking around trying to take in the unfamiliar surroundings. My parents sat to our right, my mother pleased that we were all together.

After the service began, a child several pews ahead of us who had hair the color of corn silk kept turning to look toward the back of the church, waving and smiling mischievously, as if she were trying to introduce herself to everyone, taking for granted that all would love her. Then I saw that she sat between James and Lois and my chest tightened around my heart, my mouth went dry, and the preacher seemed to stop talking.

James and Lois had recently moved back to Riverfield, but I had not expected to see them in church, or perhaps did not want to consider the possibility. But there they sat, my child no longer an abstraction, or simply a pain inside born out of my own sense of guilt. When she took communion at the rail, though, in her bright yellow dress, for one moment my guilt disappeared. How could the conception of something so beautiful be so terrible a sin?

After the service, Laura and I walked to the car with Michael between us, each of us holding one of his hands. Lois and James walked ahead, Frances beside them. As they got in their car, James turned and waved for a moment, probably unsure if he should come over and speak, or perhaps even bring Frances with him. Neither Frances nor Lois saw him wave. They merely waited for him to close his door and start the car.

Laura didn't know. She told me when we had first begun dating that she'd once heard a rumor and wanted to know if it was true. I told her that I'd heard the rumor too, and that it wasn't true. I then convinced myself that I was living up to part of my promise to never tell anyone, and that I could not go back on that promise. My ability to lie so convincingly both surprised and disgusted me. But perhaps it was so easy because Laura wanted to believe me.

There was something that Laura had not told me then that seems ironic now. While I sat there close beside Michael, looking at my daughter three pews ahead of me, Laura was already pregnant with Seth and knew it. He would be born in the fall, and I would never know a happier day. Nothing could keep me from being a father to him. I would not fail this time.

Seth

Frances and I walked down the dirt road to an old shack near her house. The roof was rusted tin and the porch steps sagged. Most of the windows were broken out, but it wasn't falling in. It looked like most of the black people's houses you see around here, only nobody had lived in it for a while. Frances said an old blind woman had lived there, that they used to take her vegetables out of the garden and see about her.

"Let's go sit on the porch," she said.

It was cold, but I was ready to do whatever she wanted.

I'd ridden my bike down after school, and this time I'd told Grandmama where I was going. Frances came to the door wearing an old work shirt and her hair was a little messed up, like she'd just gotten out of bed from a nap. She said Bobby and Johnny had gone out hunting with their daddy. "They won't be back for a while, but come on and take a walk with me," she said. I didn't mind so much then that Bobby wasn't home.

So we sat down at the top of the steps, right under the porch roof. Her shoulder kept touching me and she let me lean into her. I wanted to tell her about Michael coming by the house, but didn't know how to start. It felt strange not to be able to open my mouth and talk about my own brother, but I couldn't. He felt like another secret that had to be kept, like my mother.

But Frances must have read my mind somehow, seen inside me.

"Have you heard from your brother any?" she said.

How did you know? I wanted to say, but didn't. "He stopped by to see me the other day," I said, and that was all.

"He did?"

"I *guess* it was to see me. He didn't stay long, though."

Why not?"

"I don't know. Maybe he's mad at me."

"Why would he be mad?" she said and turned to look at me, like she was worried.

"I don't know," I said. I didn't want to tell her about the gun of his that I'd taken and thrown away. "It seems like he's almost always a little mad at me for some reason, even if he doesn't say anything mean or hit me."

"Why would he be mad at a sweet boy like you?"

I didn't want her calling me that. It made me feel like a five-year-old. "It's just the way he'll look at me or talk to me," I said. "Like I'm to blame for something."

"What are you to blame for?"

"I don't know. It's like I've done something to him."

"So what did he have to say when you saw him?"

"Not much. There didn't seem to be any reason why he came. As soon as I got home from church, he left. Out by the truck all he said was, 'How are you and your old man getting along?' I thought he must be talking about Granddaddy at first. I just said, 'Fine.' But he looked at me like he didn't believe me. Then he said a strange thing. 'He's not all he pretends. You remember that.' I don't know what he meant, but it seems like I don't understand half of what he says."

"That is strange," she said. "But don't worry about it. Maybe he just doesn't get along with your father and wants to think bad about him." She put her arm through mine then and pulled me closer to her. "What about your mama?" she said.

"What about her?"

"Did Michael say anything about her?"

"No. He didn't," I said, probably a little too quick.

"You don't have to get mad at me for asking, do you?"

"I'm not mad."

"You sound like you were maybe."

"I'm sorry."

"Do you want to see her?"

"I can't," I said after a minute.

"Why?"

"I just can't."

"Does she want to see you?"

"I guess. But I don't want to talk about her. Please don't make me."

"I think you need to see her," she said and tightened her arm around mine and squeezed hard. "Does your Daddy not want you to?"

The wind picked up then and the air blew cold against my face. I couldn't look toward Frances or say anything, but she just let me sit. After a while she took my hand. Her fingers were warm against mine, and soft. "It'll be all right," she said.

I felt like some of my secrets were out then, stolen from me, and before she could take any more of them, I pulled away from her and walked into the open field away from the house where the blind woman had lived. Frances came after me. Her steps in the tall dead weeds made a soft sound that kept getting closer and closer, and she called out to me. Her voice was as soft as the sound of her steps. "It'll be all right," she said again. I wanted to believe her, and part of me wanted to let her take all my secrets. But my mother will be dead before I see her, I thought. She'll kill herself and it'll be my fault.

Michael

My oh-so-promising career in the law came to an end on the Tuesday afternoon right after my adventure to Selma. Granddaddy was more than a little pissed off about that, but he didn't throw me out or fire me. That would have meant he hadn't succeeded, and we couldn't have that, now could we?

I thought about ways to get myself disbarred, so to speak, like going out on one of his errands and just not coming back all day, or making mistakes on all the ledger entries, but I couldn't make myself do either of those things. Finally Granddaddy sent me to the post office about three o'clock and instead of heading back to the office right away, I walked myself down to Browning and Ford's, the wholesale grocery, and got a job in the warehouse loading trucks, then went back and told him what I'd done. He nodded his head. "Perhaps that's best," he said.

"I'll start paying some rent, and I'd like to buy the truck if you'd want to sell it."

"I was wondering how long it would take before you showed initiative," he said. "Now you need to think about what you might want to do beyond loading trucks. You need a plan."

"Yes, sir," I said, but what I really needed was to get out of that damn office and get some cash in my pocket. There was something else I was in need of too, in bad need of, like any healthy young man always is. And I surely did have a plan for that. I'd been studying on it, and after I saw my father and heard what he said, I did some more studying.

Always use surprise when you can. It throws people off balance and gives you the upper hand. Doesn't matter if it's a fight you're in or a woman you're after. In some ways there's not much difference between the two. So by five that afternoon I was in Riverfield, but not to see Conrad or Seth. I went to see Frances. I'd found out where she lived the week before—that probate office is good for more than just practicing law.

Her mama answered the door. Well, not her real mama, but the woman she thought was her real mama because Frances believed the lie she'd been told, and how could your aunt in Mississippi be your mama unless your daddy was one sick son of a bitch? Unless he wasn't your daddy, which would make two lies. The more I thought about it all, the more it impressed me. And I'd already been thinking about Conrad in a whole new shiny light. Maybe he and I had a little something in common after all, and maybe we were about to have more in common.

So there I was at the back door because they've got one of those houses where when you pull in the driveway you naturally find yourself at the back of the house, just like at Seth's grandparents', and then her mama let me in while the words "back door man" ran around in my head and made me smile. There Frances sat at the kitchen table peeling carrots. Her light blond hair was pulled back and her face lit up when she saw me, like I was a hero come to save her from a life of hard work. "Surprise," I said and laughed to myself.

It was only the two of them there. Her daddy who wasn't her daddy wasn't there, and neither were her brothers who weren't really her brothers. Of course she did have a brother, but she thought that he was just a friend of her brothers, or maybe he was more than that because from what she'd told me, it sounded a little like she was trying to be his mama. It's almost just too much, isn't it?

So I ended up taking her to the store on the other side of what she called Bethel Hill. It was one hell of a climb, and then we coasted all the way down to the store. She charged the things her mama had told her to get for supper, and when we drove back up the hill, I pulled off the road at the top.

"What are you doing?" she said. Her blue eyes were about half closed and she looked like she didn't trust me.

"We're going to look at the view," I told her. "Come on."

We crossed over a fence and walked to the edge of the hill. It was some kind of view, but that wasn't what I'd come for. I knew that maybe I was pushing things along a little quick, but I took her by the hand and pulled her toward me real easy. She surrendered, just stepped right into my arms and turned her pretty face up to me with her eyes shut tight and her pale mouth barely opened. Her hands and her lips were cold at first, but she warmed. She even reached around my back then and pulled me closer. She could feel me and must have liked it because she didn't back off the way some girls will who want to pretend like a man hasn't got anything down there, like all men are their fathers. This one's mine, I thought. When the two of us got back in the truck and headed down the hill, her pressed right up against me and kissing me on the neck, I thought about Conrad and Seth and felt like some thief in the night, stealing away with a sweet young thing.

But that was just the beginning. I went to work loading trucks, and when payday came that first Friday, I had money to take her out. We went to a movie in Valhia, then drove down to lock number seven on the Black Fork. She surprised me, though. She held back, like she'd caught her breath after being on the hill and decided to slow down.

Another night, when we were down on the river again, she asked me what my plans were. I started getting a little tired of people thinking I needed a plan. Except I guess I did have a plan for Frances.

"Are you going to stay in Valhia?" she said. "Maybe look for a better job?"

"I don't know. What about you?"

"I want to go to the women's college in Columbus. I've got an aunt who went there."

"Say you do?"

"Yes."

"Do you see her much?"

"Not really. I don't think she likes it here."

"How come?" I said.

"I don't know."

Well I do, I wanted to say, but didn't.

"My mother doesn't like it around here too much either," I said.

"How come?"

"Granddaddy, I think. They didn't always get along."

"How do you and your daddy get along?"

I could feel myself tighten up when she asked that. "We do just fine," I said. Then I turned it around on her. "How do you get along with yours?" I said.

"Pretty good."

"Are you sure about that?"

"Yes. Why wouldn't I be?" She looked at me and crossed her arms and put her hands under her chin. "Sometimes you say strange things," she said. "I don't understand you."

Your father isn't your father. Your father is the man who's not my father, I wanted to say, to explain, just like I'd always wanted to tell Seth that his father wasn't my father.

She never did uncross her arms. So much for that night by the river.

Toward the end of February, when it wasn't as cold out as it had been, I took her home a little early one night.

"Let's go for a walk," I said when we pulled into the drive. She'd already told me that her mama and daddy had gone to town and that some girl was staying with her brothers.

"Okay," she said, "but let me go inside a minute."

When she came back out she'd fixed her hair a little and had taken her jacket off.

We walked out across a dead sedge field. The moon was almost full and bright as a light, and a dusk-to-dawn lamp on a pole shined from beside the road. I took her hand and she squeezed mine. Her palm was smooth and soft.

"Seth flew kites out here with me and my brothers one time," she said. "I think I probably teased him a little."

"Say you did?"

"Just a little. I think he likes the attention. I wish you'd go see him."

"Are you my mama?" I said.

We came to a dirt road that split the field and started down it. By that time we'd walked a good way from the light by the road and it was a little harder to see but not too much.

"Mama and Daddy have been drinking and fighting a lot lately," she said. "But it'll be all right for a while now."

"How do you know?"

"Because they went out tonight. That means they've made up. They probably won't raise hell for another month or so."

"Why don't they split up?"

"What do you mean?"

"Just what I said. If they don't get along, why not split?"

"Who are they going to fight with if they don't have each other?"

"That's strange."

"Not if you think about it. I don't like them fighting, but I'd hate being without either Mama or Daddy."

"Yeah, that'd be bad," I said, knowing good and well she didn't really have either one of them.

We came up on an old house then, a shack.

"Let's sit on the porch," she said.

"Anybody live there?"

"No. An old blind black woman used to, but she died."

"Well, let's go inside. I don't think she'll care much now."

"I don't know." She held back a little.

"Come on," I said and took her hand.

The front door opened up easy, and after we'd been inside for a minute and my eyes adjusted, I saw a fireplace and some junk piled in a corner. Then I took out my lighter and saw that the junk was old ragged clothes and broken up furniture.

"We got all we need," I said and took a piece of a dress and part of a chair and made a fire in the fireplace. It started right up and made a nice light for us. I sat down on the floor and looked up at her. Then I saw in her face that she was a little scared and knew what that meant. Now, I thought. It just took longer than usual.

She sat down and after a minute I pulled her up against me. Be easy, I kept telling myself. Be easy with her. I kissed her then, real soft even though I was hard enough to cut diamonds, and she opened up her mouth finally and it seemed like as the fire burned brighter she melted into me, gave in, surrendered. I unbuttoned her top real slow and took her out of it and she raised her arms and let me slip her bra off. "No further," she said. The firelight held her breasts and then I held them, took them one at a time, and she moaned so deep I knew what she said was just words. I eased her back onto the floor and found the button on her jeans. "No," she said, but it was just a word for her to be saying. I slipped my way down her and did what I don't think she even knew people ever did, and by the time I was done with that, she wasn't saying no. "God. Oh, God" was mostly it, and I felt a little like God. Then I eased my way on top of her and she turned quiet. All the way through she didn't make a sound, like she was deaf and dumb. I only heard the fire pop once or twice. Finally I

142

raised up on my arms and looked down. Her eyes were closed and her flat, white belly glowed red from the firelight. I arched my back then and pushed one last time. My arms started trembling and while I was still looking down at her body, my weight centered on her, my breath coming hard, I suddenly thought about Conrad and Seth, just like when I first kissed her. Now she's mine, I thought. Then I was done.

Laura

If a mother can't be close to her children the way she would like to be, at least she can narrow the miles. I suppose that's what I had in mind when I drove those farm-to-market roads toward Valhia, past empty cotton wagons and kudzu and run-down country stores, but it wasn't really my mind that compelled me, pushed me beyond my fears, it was my heart. Looking back, the trip was a mistake, but sometimes you have to do *something*, even if it's wrong.

I had not seen my sons for nine months, the same amount of time I carried them—actually longer than I carried Seth since he was so premature. Those months I felt as empty inside as that first moment after giving birth, before the nurse has time to hand you your child, but I filled my time with work and reading, and two nights a week I went downtown and helped adults learn to read and write, mostly older black women who reminded me of the women that used to come into Valhia on Saturdays when I was a child. I'd had to do something to fight off depression, had to keep it at bay as best as I knew how. No more doctors. Never again that taste of black rubber and the clinched wait for what would come.

Daddy was surprised to see me. I hadn't told him I was coming. I simply left work early Friday afternoon. I hadn't seen him since that last weekend with Seth, a long time to go without a visit, but we'd talked over the phone and written. Perhaps the reason for my staying away was the very same one that drew me home—I couldn't stand being so cut off from my children.

We sat downstairs and talked while it grew dark outside and our reflections grew stronger against the large windows.

"I don't know where Michael is," he said. "He never tells me. He only says he's going 'out.' Since he's grown, I don't ask."

"If you did ask, he probably wouldn't tell you. Or he'd lie."

Daddy only nodded his head at first, then said finally, "He is difficult at times."

"More than I was?" I said, hoping for some slight smile, but none came.

"You made some mistakes. You were young."

"And stupid?"

"That's not the word I'd use. Don't be so hard on yourself."

He must have seen the surprised look on my face, must have known what I was thinking.

"Maybe I was the difficult one, the one who was stupid. Since your mother's been gone, I've thought a great deal about the things she tried to say to me."

"Well I guess I'll see Michael when I see him," I said, not knowing how to respond really to what he'd just said. The only real thought that occurred to me then was that it had already become dark outside and only because of the darkness could I now see us so clearly in our reflection against the glass.

The next morning I was sitting at the small desk in the kitchen where Mother used to write letters, and where she gave herself insulin shots, when Michael walked in. He'd come home too late the night before for me to see him, but he must have known I was there since my car was parked in the driveway. He had on a pair of shorts that he'd probably slept in, and no shirt. He looked healthy. He was trim and his arms and chest looked muscular, and his eyes had light in them, not anger or the far away stare I'd seen too often. He pulled at the bottom of his shorts, like a little boy.

"How are you, Mama?" he said.

I stood up and hugged him tight, and it felt good to feel his skin, to be that close to him.

"You look good," I said.

"I've been working hard."

"So I hear. I'm glad you're with your grandfather, glad you're not down in Florida anymore. But mostly I'm just glad to see you."

"Well," he said, and shrugged. That was all. A way of dismissing our last words to each other, to say, Let's make a truce.

He went to the refrigerator and poured himself some orange juice.

"Why don't you take a shower?" I said. "And I'll fix us all some breakfast."

He drank, then put down the glass. "That sounds good," he said and nodded. "I am a little hungry."

So I fixed a big breakfast, and it felt familiar to me, comfortable, like an old ritual that I was performing in my mother's kitchen, using her pans and plates and bowls, cooking the way she cooked. When we sat at the table, it felt so different from the last time we'd eaten together, after Mother's funeral when Michael and I had been arguing. Daddy told me about some of the people I'd gone to school with—who'd moved away, who'd come back, who'd remarried. I asked Michael about his job. He said it felt good doing physical work again, then added, with an easy grin, that of course there was nothing wrong with office work, and my father smiled. "I think we're in full agreement on that point," he said. "Nothing wrong with a little physical work, either. It's good for the soul, or so I hear." Then he chuckled.

Soon I began to feel as if something were missing, though. It wasn't my mother because I somehow felt her presence. Then I realized that it was, of course, Seth. Daddy and Michael seemed to sense the change in my mood, the quietness that came over me, and after we'd eaten Michael said he would take care of the dishes. I was a little shocked at his offer, but touched. He must have seen my shock. "Well I do know how to wash dishes," he said and smiled that crooked smile from the corner of his mouth that, this time, was only charming.

Later Michael left and was gone all day, and my father and I took a drive around town, not something I was sure about doing, but he seemed anxious to get out and go somewhere. I generally don't like exercises in nostalgia, and this turned out to be no exception. We drove past the little house on Church Street where I grew up. The pines in the front looked larger and the house smaller, not kept up as well, but perhaps it was just time to paint.

We drove past some property outside of town that my father was interested in, then headed back into town, past my old high school where I learned the important arts of baton twirling and flirting, and we finally drove through the quarters behind the house, coming in the back way. Poor black children played on the hard-packed dirt in front of the houses my father rented, and they stopped to look at us as if we had the answer to some question they didn't know how to ask. One boy who looked about twelve or thirteen stopped bouncing the basketball they'd been playing with, tucked it under his arm, and stared right at me. He seemed lost, and I couldn't help but wonder if he had a mother at home. "Seth. I want to try to see him," I said suddenly, realizing that perhaps *this* was why I'd come.

I called from Mother's desk, praying Conrad would be the one to answer the phone, and when I heard his formal and resonant voice, I asked if we could see one another and talk. He was taken aback at hearing from me, and sounded a little leery, but he agreed without asking why.

We met at the small park next to our old high school and across the road from the cemetery. He looked a little thinner, and he walked slowly as he approached, as if he'd been injured maybe. His face was tired. He was, I saw, more afraid than me.

From the bench where we sat down I could see the football field, the school library, and the hill across the road where Mother was buried, even the statue of the town's Confederate soldier standing on its pedestal near the cemetery entrance. Somehow it all seemed so appropriate, and as hard to take as the words Conrad spoke.

"I know you miss him," he said. "But not now."

"Is he all right?"

"Yes. He's made some friends. He's healthy."

"What about school?"

"His grades are good, but he puts too much pressure on himself."

"He's always done that. Is it worse?"

"Maybe. A little. And he's sullen sometimes. Hard to reach," he said. "But I guess that's understandable."

"Yes. I guess it would be, wouldn't it?"

He raised his eyebrows and looked at me, then sighed.

"Does he say anything about me? Ask about me?" I knew these were dangerous questions, but I had to ask them.

"No. To be honest we don't talk about you."

"Not at all?"

"No."

"I'm like the old crone in the attic in some bad gothic novel?"

"You're the one who reads fiction."

"That's right. How's the War coming? Is the honorable South losing again?"

"Sarcasm never has become you, Laura."

I pulled back then, softened my voice and tried again. "Conrad, I know you're a decent man. You always have to do what's 'right.' You know he needs to see me, and you know why he won't ask to."

He looked at me genuinely puzzled. "Not now," he said. "I'm sorry. He can't handle it right now."

"Do you really think I was that terrible a mother?"

He looked away from me. "I'll let you know if things change."

He stood then and walked away, slowly, his posture rigid. When he passed from under an oak and into the late afternoon sun, the harsh light hit him and seemed to illuminate for me all of his failings, and in his failings, I saw my own.

Daddy and I ate a light supper. He didn't press me for any details about my meeting with Conrad, for which I was grateful. I sat up reading in Mother's old chair until very late that night, then Michael came in.

"Hello there, Mother," he said and stood over my chair.

Mother was the tip off. He never calls me that.

"I'm glad you made it home," I said, hoping to keep any edge of sarcasm out of my voice.

"Did you doubt that your wandering son would come home?"

"I really hadn't thought about it. I assumed you would."

"I might not have. I was in some pretty good company. Or maybe I should say some pretty company."

"And who would that have been?"

"Just a young lady," he said and smiled his father's crooked smile. The smell of alcohol grew stronger as he talked. "You might say I've been seeing a lot of her lately. A whole lot."

"I don't need to know the details of your exploits with women."

"You might want to know about this woman."

"Michael, this is getting old, and I really don't care."

"I may have to be leaving soon. I don't know yet."

"Back to Florida?"

"Maybe California. Maybe Timbuktu."

"Why will you be leaving? You don't sound sure."

"If things go like I expect they will, I'll sure be headed out of here."

With that he walked to his room and made two false steps, which meant he was very drunk.

Seth

Bobby took me out on the slough off the Black Fork River, where his father had a boat hidden up on the bank. The weather was starting to get warmer and I'd ridden my bike down to his house early that Saturday. We turned the boat right side up and watched careful for snakes, then slid the boat into the water and climbed in. Bobby sat in back, and I took the front. Both of us had a paddle. They'd been up under the boat, along with the two cane fishing poles we planned on using. We'd already hunted for nightcrawlers under dried manure and had found a good many.

The slough looked pretty swampy, and we paddled across it to a place where there were a lot of stumps and logs in the water. It looked like a good place to fish.

"It might be too cold still for the fish to bite. But it'll give us something to do," Bobby said. "Beats staying around the house waiting on Daddy to come back and put us to work."

"Where was everybody?" I said.

"Mama and Daddy both went to town. Johnny went with them."

"What about Frances?"

"Miss Priss was still in bed. She was out late last night. She's been seeing somebody, but he don't never come around the house. At least I know I ain't seen him. Mama and Daddy don't like her going out with him, best I can tell."

I'd hoped she would come with us, but didn't say it. Bobby would have wanted to know why, and I don't know what I would have told him. I was glad to hear she was home though. Maybe she would still be there when we went back.

We baited our hooks and then watched our corks on the water and didn't talk for a while. The boat drifted along with the current, and Bobby finally tied us to an old dead tree sticking up out of the water. It was gray and rotted without any limbs, but still tall. The sun kept going behind the clouds and made the slough look darker than it did already from the blackness of the water and from the shadows of the trees that grew down to the bank.

We listened to a mockingbird, and Bobby said, "I don't know what's gotten into Mama and Daddy lately." He said it like he'd been waiting to say it.

"What do you mean?"

"They ain't been fighting like normal."

"But they don't always fight, do they?"

"No, but when they ain't fighting, they're usually happy."

"They're not happy now?"

"Don't seem like it. Something's going on. I don't know what. Was your parents ever like that?"

"All the time," I said.

We sat there quiet again. A turtle pushed off a log and into the dark water, and our corks floated still as they could be. Clouds like rows of plowed ground stopped over us and hid the sun again, and that made it a little cold.

"Looks like it's too early in the year to catch fish," Bobby said.

A big white crane flew in over the trees then and landed at the very top of the dead tree we were tied to. It flexed its wings a few times, and they looked as white as anything ever could above that black water and gray trunk, whiter than a house just painted. I started thinking about Frances then and saw her face.

152

At least you've got Frances, I wanted to say to Bobby. You're lucky.

We got back to Bobby's house in time to eat lunch. There weren't any fish on our stringer, but at least that meant we didn't have any to clean. His mama and daddy were home by then, and his mama fixed a place for me at the table. Then his daddy came in and we all sat down. At first I thought Frances must have been gone, but there was an empty chair and a plate in front of it.

"Y'all dig in," his mama said. "She'll be on directly." Not that anybody but me was waiting.

"Why's she late all the time now?" their daddy said.

Their mama didn't answer. Nobody else said anything either.

Then she came walking in. She acted like she was tired. She kept blinking her eyes. Her mama just looked at her.

"Good morning," her daddy said. "You get enough beauty sleep?"

She didn't answer, and when she sat down it was like she'd just seen me.

"Hey, Seth," she said, then smiled.

We ate ham and potato salad and stuffed eggs. Nobody said much. I could see what Bobby meant. Things weren't the same.

"We didn't catch any fish," Bobby said, trying to get people to talk it seemed like.

"You ought to take Seth where he can *catch* fish," Frances said. "Be good to your company." She smiled again. "Tell him, Seth."

I didn't know what to say, so I just nodded my head and looked at the table.

"Has that cat got your tongue again?"

"No," I said. "I thought we might catch some there."

"How's your daddy, Seth?" their mama said before Frances could say anything else.

"He's fine."

"How about your brother?"

Bobby's daddy looked at her funny after she said that, like he didn't want her bringing up Michael.

"He's fine too," I said. "I haven't seen him in a while, though."

"He's living in town now, ain't he? In Valhia?"

"Yes, ma'am."

"But you or your daddy ain't seen him?"

"Not lately."

"Seems like y'all would want to see him. Doesn't he like to visit?" She smiled like she knew something I didn't.

Frances stared at her mama. Her mouth was open like she was about to say something ugly.

"Why don't you let Seth eat and not ask the boy so many questions?" their daddy said.

"I'm making polite conversation, that's all." She looked at him, then at Frances, like there was a secret between the three of them.

"Just let the boy eat." He tried to smile at me after he said it, but it wasn't a real smile. He was trying to help me, though.

Bobby kept looking at me, trying to let me know not to worry about anything, probably. I wondered if he knew about whatever was going on. It didn't seem like he did. His mama was talking about my brother, but I didn't know how she knew Michael was in Valhia, or how she knew anything about him at all.

I had a hard time eating. Every bite made me feel a little sick, and I wouldn't look at their mama anymore, just at Bobby and Frances. She kept staring at her mama.

When we finished eating, their daddy stood up. "Frances, why don't you get the truck and take these boys fishing down at The Landing?" he said. "Take them to the point at the end of the road and see what y'all catch."

It looked like she started to say she didn't want to, but then said, "Yes, sir."

Bobby and I put four fishing poles in the back of the truck, and

Bobby made Johnny get in the cab. He complained, but Bobby told him somebody had to ride up front. Then Bobby and I climbed into the back of the truck and waited for Frances.

She came out the back door and slammed it hard, then walked to the truck. "They're about to fight," she said. "I mean really fight."

"Don't you know it," Bobby said. "What are they going to fight about?"

"I don't know," Frances said. But she did. I could tell.

She drove us up the Loop Road, past Jackson Quarter, then onto the highway. The wind in the back of the truck got a little cool, but not too bad. She turned pretty fast onto the dirt road that goes to The Landing and didn't slow down much even though there were a lot of ruts and loose gravel all the way to the river. She drove like she was mad still.

After she got stopped, Bobby and Johnny and I started down the hill to the water, each of us carrying a pole. Johnny had the can of worms. But Frances wasn't behind us. She was sitting on top of a picnic table, the same one the two of us had sat on once.

"Ain't you coming?" Bobby said.

"In a little while."

"Suit yourself," Bobby said and rolled his eyes.

We walked out to the end of the point and baited up and put our lines in. It was the same as at the slough for a while. Then Johnny caught a bream, but not one big enough to keep.

Frances kept walking to the edge of the hill and would look down at us. Then she'd disappear back over the edge. I wondered what she was doing. Finally I told Bobby to watch my cork. He probably thought I was going to look for a place to pee, but I climbed the hill and found Frances sitting on top of the picnic table looking down the road we'd come in on like she was waiting on somebody. I went and sat beside her, wishing it was like before when we sat at the same table—just the two of us, without Bobby and Johnny nearby.

"You don't want to fish?" I said.

"No. Not today."

"Is something wrong?"

She hadn't been crying, but she might as well have been for how she looked in her eyes.

"Mama's a bitch," she said.

I'd heard her cuss before, but not that word and not so strong in the way she said it. Something moved inside me, like she'd said something dirty. I knew it was a terrible thing to say about your mother.

"What's wrong?" I said. "Why are your parents mad? Are they mad at you?"

She glanced at me and I could see that she knew the answers, but that she wasn't going to tell me. People want to hide everything, keep secrets, but they can't do it forever. Still, they try. Michael tries to make everything a secret. Now Frances had one, and it was hurting her. Secrets always hurt. You want to tell them but you can't, and then when people do tell, everybody else gets to hurt.

"Mama's just acting ugly. She's mad at Daddy about something and wants to make everybody miserable."

"But what's she mad about?"

"I don't know. Something."

She smiled then, but it was like she was trying to cover up her real face.

"So how have you been? I haven't seen you much lately," she said.

"I'm okay."

"How's school?"

"It's okay, too."

"Is there any girl there you like? Somebody cute?"

"No. Not really," I said, which was true, mostly. I looked at her then and noticed how much longer her hair was getting, how soft it looked against her neck, and I knew that I had something to hide too.

"Well, you'll find some cute girl to like," she said and took my hand. "Come on, let's walk down the hill."

We got up from the table and while she led me, I thought to myself that she hadn't asked about Michael. She usually did, and it seemed like she would have after her mama brought him up the way she did.

We fished some more, but not Frances. She just watched. I caught a small bass and threw it back. Then Bobby caught a good-sized one. "I'm eating this for supper," he said.

After we left, Frances dropped me off at my house. Bobby and I rode in the back again, Johnny up front. I got out on Frances' side and she stuck her head out of the window and said bye and winked at me, but it was slow and sad, like whatever the wink was about couldn't be a good thing.

I turned and walked under the carport, and Daddy was standing on the porch and waving as Frances pulled away. He looked like something was bothering him.

"Where's your bike?" he said.

"It's still down at Bobby's," I told him. "We went fishing and Frances told me she'd bring it by tomorrow maybe."

"Okay."

"Is something wrong?" I said.

He didn't seem like he heard me at first. "No," he finally said. "Nothing."

Instead of Frances bringing my bike the next day, Bobby and his mama did. They didn't stay but a minute, and his mama didn't get out of the truck even. She just smoked a cigarette and kept the motor running while Bobby and I lifted the bike from the truck bed.

But Frances did come by the next Saturday while I sat out on the back porch cleaning my pellet gun. She pulled up in her mama's white Ford. It was late in the afternoon, and I was at home by myself because Grandmama had run to town and Daddy was at the store with Granddaddy.

"Have you been shooting birds?" She sat down beside me like she wasn't sure if she should or not. Something didn't seem natural about her.

"No. Not today. What have you been doing?"

"I've been out just driving around and thought I'd stop by for a minute. I can't stay." Her voice sounded strange, like she didn't want to talk at all.

So we sat there for a while and I oiled my gun with a rag. I could hear big trucks pass out on the highway. Then she got up finally and walked around under the carport. I kept thinking that she had something important to tell me. I was waiting to hear, but didn't know how to ask.

"Maybe I shouldn't have come," she said. "I've really got to go. I'll see you later, okay?" She started walking to her car, but she stopped and turned around and walked back up to where I sat. She leaned down toward me and I felt her hair brush across my face and a perfume like dogwood flowers filled the air. Then I felt her lips warm against my cheek. "Bye," she said and walked back toward her car.

At school on Monday Bobby told me that Frances had left to go live with their aunt in Mississippi. He said he didn't really know why, that his mama and daddy hadn't explained it in any way that made good sense, but that she was sure gone. Then he said something that hit me harder than what he'd just told me. "Your brother came by the house on Friday after school," he said. "Looks like he's the one who she's been seeing. I don't think Mama and Daddy like him too much."

That afternoon I left my books at school, walked right past the bus, and started toward downtown. A couple of girls asked me where I was going, but I didn't say a word to them. I made it to the Square, then walked to Granddaddy's office. Some woman was behind the front desk and before I could ask where Michael was, Granddaddy came out of his office.

"Seth," he said. "I'm glad to see you." He shook my hand and even put his other hand on my shoulder.

"Where's Michael?" I said.

"He's been working down at Browning and Ford's. Why don't you come back in my office and sit a few minutes. I'm not too busy right now. I've missed seeing you."

"No, sir. I really need to see Michael," I said.

So I left the office and walked down Scott Street and past the train tracks. I didn't know what I was going to say to him exactly. All I could do was picture him with Frances and think about the way he would have treated her and the things he probably did to her. I knew what he did with women. I remembered how he'd looked at Frances that first time and said she had a nice ass. Then Frances came into my mind, and I wondered why she would let him or even want to see him at all and I was mad at her too, especially for not telling me anything, and then I got even madder at Michael. But why did she have to leave? I kept wondering, then told myself, She's just your friend's sister, that's all. But that wasn't all. I felt so bad, as bad as at Grandmama's funeral, and I couldn't believe Frances was gone. Then I thought about Mama, how far away she was and how long it had been since I'd seen her. I felt as empty and hurting inside as when you're sick and wanting your mama but too ashamed to let anybody know it.

Several trucks were backed up to the loading dock at Browning and Ford's, and I saw two black men standing beside a handtruck when I made it up the steps. They looked like they were on a break. One was smoking a cigarette, the other was talking.

"Can y'all tell me where Michael is?" I said.

Before either one could answer, Michael walked up.

"Well, hello there, little brother. I was going to come see you today."

"You were?" I said, so surprised that I didn't know what else to say.

"Looks like I'm leaving town. Thought I'd come say good-bye."

"Frances has left."

"She has?" He nodded his head real slow, like he expected that.

"What did you do to her?"

He took the pack of cigarettes from his shirt pocket and lit one with his silver lighter and took a deep drag. He just looked at me real calm and didn't answer.

"You've been seeing her?"

"Sure have," he said. "You didn't know that? I thought she'd tell you."

"Why's she left? What happened?"

He blew a long stream of smoke from the corner of his mouth. "I think you already know," he said, "or at least have a guess. You're old enough. You know what goes on between men and women."

"She's pregnant," I said. It was the first time I'd let myself think it, and I knew it was true as soon as I said it. "And you're leaving?"

"People don't always get married when it happens." He took another long drag off his cigarette. "It'll be taken care of," he said finally. "Believe me, there's a lot of people to help Frances. Maybe I'll even send her some money sometime."

"But you don't have any."

"Not right now, I don't, but I've got plans."

"What are they?"

He shook his head and wouldn't tell me.

"Do you know where Frances went?"

160

"To Mississippi, Bobby said, to live with her aunt."

"That makes sense. More sense than she probably even knows."

"I'll miss her," I said. "She was my friend."

"That's the way it goes sometimes," he said and shrugged his shoulders, like none of this meant anything or mattered, like Frances didn't matter. Or me.

I wanted to hurt him then. I wanted to punch him in the face.

"I've got to get back to work," he said and held out his hand. I wouldn't take it. "All right then, if that's the way you want it." He walked back into the warehouse and disappeared past the stacks of brown boxes and the forklifts and the men pushing handtrucks.

I didn't know when I'd see him again, or even if I wanted to.

Conrad

Seth called me at work and told me that he had missed the school bus. The odd thing was that his call came far past the time school got out, but I didn't think about that until after he hung up, probably because of all that was going on in my mind at the moment. James had come in to see me before Seth's call and what he'd had to tell me was almost more than I could take in, yet somehow I wasn't shocked.

But for the moment Seth had to be taken care of and I tried to concentrate on him while I drove from Demarville to Valhia. He'd said he would wait on the Square, and that's where I found him, standing near the probate office. He looked very tall against the side of the white stucco building; and perhaps because he didn't carry any books, or perhaps because of the angry, even cold, expression he wore, he didn't look at all like a school-boy who'd missed the bus, but more like some rough kid who couldn't wait to quit school and spend time loafing around town. Then, just as I decided my imagination was running away with me, I realized that what I was really seeing in him, probably for the first time, was a trace of his brother, and that scared me a little.

"Did you call from school?" I asked when he climbed into the car.

"No, sir. I called from Granddaddy's office."

This news surprised me greatly, but I didn't let on. "How is he?"

"Fine."

"Did you see Michael?"

"No. He's not working for Granddaddy any more."

"Where's he working? He is still in town, isn't he?"

"He's loading trucks at Browning and Ford's, Granddaddy said."

"But you didn't see Michael?"

"No, sir," he said.

He was quiet on the way home and I couldn't help but think that something was wrong. Why had he walked all the way from school to his grandfather's office to call me? That didn't make sense. And why had his face looked so hard? Somehow I felt that maybe Seth knew what Michael had done. I thought again about James coming to see me earlier. "Jack's boy been seeing her. He's the father," James had said. "Don't hold you responsible. I know he ain't your boy."

Michael and I were now father and grandfather to the same child, and something told me that, oddly enough, Michael had accomplished this by design.

May

Son went to see Michael at Mr. Tyner's after we ate supper. He felt like he had to. While he was gone Seth came into the kitchen where I was making a pound cake.

"Daddy went to see Michael, didn't he?"

"Yes," I said. "How did you know?"

"I heard y'all talking in here before supper."

"Do you know why he went to see him?"

"Not exactly, but I don't think Michael will be there."

"How do you know?"

"I went to see Michael after school."

"That's why you missed the bus?"

"Yes, ma'am. And Michael told me he was leaving."

"Do you know why?"

"Yes, ma'am. Frances."

"Did you know that Frances is gone?"

"Yes, ma'am."

"And you know why?"

"Yes, ma'am," he said.

"You like her, don't you?"

He nodded his head, like he was embarrassed.

"More than you like Bobby?"

"I don't know," he said then. "It's different. She's different."

164

Yes, I thought. She is. I was only glad he couldn't know how different, and part of me was relieved she was gone.

"Michael hasn't been a very good brother to you, has he?"

"No, ma'am," he said, and I could see the hurt, see it in the way he looked at the floor and frowned.

"Sometimes brothers aren't good to each other. Look in the Bible, at all the old stories. Sometimes family can hurt you more than anyone," I said, and then realized just how true he knew that was.

I was so worried about him, and prayed for him each night. He was already without his mother. Now his brother was probably gone after doing so much harm, and Frances was gone. I was also worried about something else. Son had started seeing a woman in Demarville, and he hadn't told Seth yet. I didn't know if this news would bother him or not, but figured that it would. I suppose Son did too. But it was nothing Seth needed to know about at the moment.

June–August 1976

May

Marriage is hard sometimes, especially if you don't marry well. Conrad and I have been married a long time now, and there have certainly been difficult times, like when the old wooden store burned in '59 and we were already about to build the new house. I had been wanting a new house for years, and suddenly it didn't look like I'd ever have one. But Conrad built a new store and a year later built a new house. He made me happy.

Sometimes people just aren't right for each other, though, and maybe don't know each other long enough, or well enough, before they marry. And sometimes people don't get married for the right reason. They just fool themselves into thinking it's love when it's not because they really want something else, like somebody to take care of them.

So when Son took up with seeing Kate, the woman from Demarville, I hoped he wasn't looking to get married again, at least not for a long time. I hoped he'd be real careful about the woman he picked. Then he brought her by to meet us on a Sunday for noon dinner, and that's when I got worried and thought it might be serious.

She was friendly enough, and pretty enough. She said she was from Mississippi, but had been in Nashville for a long time. An aunt and some cousins lived in Demarville. That was how she ended up here. And she had a job as a secretary, she said.

When we all sat down at the table that day, she told us she had a daughter named Erin, about a year younger than Seth. I sure hoped Son wouldn't marry her then. Not another one with a child, I thought.

I really put out the food. I'd cooked a roast and a casserole, and there were snap beans and corn and both rolls and cornbread. A custard pie was cooling on the kitchen counter for dessert. I hadn't even gone to Sunday school that morning getting it all ready.

Seth said the blessing after I asked him to. Then we passed the food around. Kate was careful not to take too much of anything and ate real small bites. I don't think she liked the casserole, though. She just pushed at it with her fork. I asked her about Nashville, how she'd liked it up there, and she said that Erin had gone to a good public school and that she'd worked at a music company.

"Did you have a church up there?" I asked her then.

"Well . . ." Kate said, and it didn't look like she knew what else to say. Her eyes got a little wide. "We went to a Methodist church sometimes," she finally said. Then she took a bite of roast and when she was done chewing she said, as quick as she could, how good it was.

Son said a little something now and then, but not Seth. He was quiet. It looked like maybe he was curious about things. He'd look at his daddy, then at Kate, maybe wondering just who this woman was that his daddy had brought home. And she'd ask him something every once in a while, like how he liked school. She was uneasy with him. He answered politely, but no more than that. He probably could have done a little better, to tell the truth.

Finally I served up the pie, and when we were done, Kate offered to help do the dishes. Of course I wouldn't hear of that. I said I'd do them later. We all sat down in the living room then

170

and tried to visit for a while. Seth must have gone back to his room, but he came back out right before Kate left.

Son was going to drive her back to Demarville, and I just happened to catch a glimpse of them through a window after they went outside. They were standing by his car talking and all of a sudden she gave him a mean look and he shook his head and said something back to her. Then she turned away from him and her lips were pressed tight together. They finally got in the car and drove off. I never did know what they were mad about, and I never did tell Conrad about it.

That night before bed, Conrad asked me what I thought of her. "She seems all right," I said.

"You think he's going to marry her?"

"Might," I said. "But he hasn't made any announcement yet. We'll just have to wait and see."

A few weeks later, or about that long, Son asked Conrad about the old house, where we all used to live. He wanted to know how much we'd sell it for. He said he'd like to buy it from us and fix it up whenever we could get the renters out. That's when I knew for sure.

Months later the wedding day arrived, a Saturday. Seth stood good and straight and to the right of his daddy at the front of the Episcopal church, and Kate's daughter Erin was just to her left. On the altar above them, Father Rhodes, a distinguished looking older gentleman, stood dressed in his collar and a white robe. Kate wore a nice cream-colored dress and her daughter, who looked very pretty, a peach one. I can't say her daughter was all that friendly, really. Seth looked nice. I'd taken him to Demarville a few weeks before to buy a new gray suit, and new shoes.

There weren't many people attending. Son wanted to keep it small and simple. The Episcopal church wasn't his idea, though. It was hers. We weren't Episcopalian, though we sometimes attended with friends, and she wasn't Episcopalian either. But she saw the old church and thought it was charming and wanted to know if they could get permission to marry there.

It certainly would have been cooler in the Methodist church with the air conditioner on. I knew the first of June would be hot, and it surely was. The doors were open, both in back and on the side, but the high ceiling seemed like it only allowed room for more heat to collect. I dabbed at my face with a handkerchief, and Seth kept wiping his forehead with the tips of his fingers trying to keep the perspiration out of his eyes.

Neither Conrad or I thought Son had waited long enough before he asked her. But we didn't try to talk him out of it. I was concerned for him and for Seth, concerned about what kind of a wife she'd be and how she'd treat Seth. It was just a feeling I had. I suppose there are times I take a satisfaction in being proved right, but this time I hoped I was wrong. No mother wants to see her son suffer, and no grandmother wants to see her grandboy hurt.

So they exchanged rings and finished saying their vows. Then everyone walked outside to the front of the church and milled around and talked for a few minutes. There were about twenty of us, including Kate's parents and a sister from Mississippi. Seemed like nice people.

The reception was at the old house, where Son had been doing some work trying to get the place clean and ready for them to move into. I'd decorated a table and seen to the cake and cookies and punch. When I got there I finished getting everything out. It all looked nice, nothing elaborate, though.

Kate and Son had their picture made with the cake, and then there were a few more made with Seth and Erin in them. Seth smiled for all the pictures, but I don't know how he felt about having a stepmother and a stepsister. He hadn't seemed excited about his daddy getting married, but it had gotten so hard to tell how he felt about anything. He'd been spending a lot more time alone, off down in the pasture, or riding his bike, and he hadn't gone down to see Bobby since the trouble with Michael. Of course, I felt it was best that he didn't go to see Bobby. And I never asked him how Bobby was, even though I knew he saw him at school.

After the last of the pictures were made and we were all eating cake, Kate started apologizing, first for how hot it had been in church, and then she said, "I think it's even hotter in this house. We'll just have to put in air conditioning right away." She said it to some Nashville friend of hers, and I don't know what it was, something in her tone, like we didn't know about air conditioning down here, and all I could think was, I lived in this house many a year without it. You can stand it for a little while. But of course she was right. It was very uncomfortable.

What really did make me mad, though, was when I overheard her tell the same friend that she wished the reception had been catered. That just didn't make sense, not for such a small wedding as it was, and I thought I'd taken care of things just fine.

Later on, after they'd been married awhile, I heard her say, and saw her do, a lot of things that didn't make sense.

When the reception was over, they left for a short honeymoon down at Gulf Shores. Erin stayed with her cousins, and Seth stayed his last few days in the house with us. I knew it would be a little something of a relief not to have to wash his clothes and cook for him, and for his daddy, but I also knew how much I'd miss seeing him every morning and every night, how much I'd miss the sound of his quick steps coming in and out of the back door.

Conrad

I had been working on the old house for weeks before the wedding, not trying to do major repairs, which I knew were needed and would take skilled labor, but just little things like cleaning and painting here and there and moving in the few items of furniture that I'd had in storage, and also furniture from out of Kate's apartment. I put in a new stove and refrigerator, too. Seth and I could have gone ahead and moved in, but I wanted to wait until after the honeymoon when we could all move in together. I suppose I thought of it as a beginning and, in a way, perhaps the repairs to be done would be more than just work on an old house, maybe even more than just repairs. I felt that perhaps something new could be built, a history begun in a house that already had its own history. I wanted life inside the house to be as solid and stable as I knew the old house was at its very core.

It was built before the War, in 1840, the same year my great-grandfather was born, the man who would one day run away from Durham, North Carolina, and end up here only a few years before the War would begin. The builder was a Mr. Rogers, who was married but had no children, only a few servants. He was not rich, and he didn't build any planter's mansion, but he built a fine house with three large bedrooms, a good-sized dining room, and a long front porch, which has always had the

174

customary swing and scuppernong vine growing between two columns.

The house came into my family when my grandmother and grandfather bought it in 1904. My father, their only child, was born in the middle bedroom, the same room where I was born. Then my grandfather died in 1913 from pneumonia, at least that's what Grandmother always told me. Years later I found out that he died from what may have been whiskey poisoning. When my father was grown my grandmother remarried, and when her second husband died she moved in with us. I was probably only about a year old at the time.

There was always someone around the house. When my mother taught school, Grandmother was home, and Leathy Ann, the cook, was in the kitchen. I would play at her feet and listen to her sing what I later learned were Negro spirituals. All I knew when I was a child was that she sang about Jesus and chariots, and "coming in at the door." She was surely blessed in her abilities to cook. Other than Leathy Ann, there was Major, who cut firewood and stovewood and tended the garden and patched the chicken coops and did whatever else needed doing around the place. Later my father bought the farm behind the house and grew cotton, then, in the years to come, raised cattle. The help he hired to work on the place were often at the house.

Each day while my father was up at the store and either my mother or grandmother were seeing to the running of the house, I spent my time playing in my sandpile beneath the giant pecan tree that grew at the edge of the yard, or some days I might go down in the pasture and walk along the creek. After lunch I would often make my way up to the store and watch the people come in and out, or I'd go and watch Ned, the blacksmith, hammer a piece of iron into shape.

So much has changed over the years, so much lost, but that old life lives in my memory and sometimes seems more real to me than anything since. I know that this is a faulty way of looking at the world. People have felt the need to pronounce this to me, sometimes with great anger, people such as Laura, or my mother, as if they are always able to see the world as it really is, see it past a need to be right.

For better or worse, I have attempted to make Seth see what the world used to be like, my world, anyway. I've wanted to give him some sense of the past, to let him know where he came from and who he is. I suppose there are other ways of achieving some sense of yourself, such as finding work you enjoy and that's meaningful to you, or finding a woman to love and to build a family with, but those ways, important as they are, don't seem enough somehow. They don't go deep enough, far enough back, and they can take so long to discover. Your own history does not change. You can only explore it more deeply, and what you learn, including the things that surprise you, can better tell you who you are, even if they might have to do with events that took place long before you were born.

When I first showed Kate the house, she wanted to know its history. She asked questions, wanted to know about my life there, or at least it seemed as if she did. I drove her all over the countryside, showing her the other towns nearby, the old ante-bellum homes, just the kind of thing Laura never enjoyed. We took any number of Sunday drives, but we never went anywhere on Saturdays, that was time I left open for Seth, in case he wanted to do something. Often he didn't. But Saturday nights Kate and I went out, maybe to eat or to Tuscaloosa to a movie.

In fact, we met on a Saturday night at a party in Demarville. Not that I usually go to parties, but this one was small, really just a dinner party. She was so lively and pretty, and she talked to me about her daughter toward the end of the evening, about prob-lems her daughter was having at school. I could hear the concern in her voice as she told me she wasn't sure what to do, and I re-member thinking that she must be a good mother. That's what really impressed me. I'd been out with a few other women, but

Kate was the only one who wanted to talk about children. Perhaps the other women had been afraid that the subject of children wasn't a wise one with a man, even if he had a child.

So Kate and I began seeing each other, and then the idea of marrying again came into my mind. It was at that point when I first drove her past the old house. I was already beginning to imagine what it would be like to live in it again, what it would be like for the four of us. There would be no Leathy Ann or Major, nor Grandmother, but I knew that I would be able to hear the echo of their voices within those walls, and that I would be able to watch Seth and Erin wait for the school bus on the front porch just as I used to, or see them wander down the hill into the pasture or up to the store for a Coke, and there would be a woman's presence in the house when they returned, or rather a mother's presence.

We married six weeks after I proposed, and two years after my divorce.

Then we moved in. Kate and I took the front bedroom, which was my old room, Erin the middle bedroom, where my father and I were born, and Seth the back bedroom. One of the first things I had to do was replace the old swing. Erin was sitting in it when the bottom cracked. I told her it wasn't her fault. Then Kate said she thought it would be nice if the porch were more open and asked if the scuppernong vine could come down. I thought about all the times I used to hide behind it as a child and spy on people as they walked along the road in front of the house, pretending to myself that they were some kind of enemy; but I wanted to please Kate, and after a few days of thinking about it, I went and bought a bush axe. After that I cleared the back and side yard, which had grown up in brush.

A driveway had to be put in, too. We had always parked beside the road in front, or even in the yard beneath the two tall oak trees, but that really wasn't very satisfactory. We needed a drive at the end of the house. The only problem was that the giant pecan that I used to play under would have to be cut down and its stump and roots pushed up. There was no telling how old it might have been, but I had it done; and while the men did the cutting, and later when the bulldozer and grader did their work, I felt as if my childhood were being erased.

I finally got started on the real work that had to be done on the house. The old plaster walls and ceilings were cracked and chipped, badly in some rooms, and there was absolutely no insulation anywhere in the house. I wasn't sure what to do at first, but I finally met with a contractor and made plans to add closets and a bathroom and to lower the high ceilings and to put up sheetrock walls against the old plaster ones, with insulation placed between the walls and ceilings to make it possible to heat the house comfortably. The problem was that the rooms would not look the same, and I felt as if I were making plans to seal up the house I'd grown up in behind something false, but the work had to be done.

Before we moved in, I'd noticed that the floor in the hall sagged a little toward one end, and back near the kitchen too, in the alcove just off the back porch. I knew that I'd have to get under the house and take a look, and that some bracing would have to be done before the work inside could begin. What I found made me sick in my stomach, and in my heart. The old hand-hewn sills and joists, which had been made by slaves, were so rotten beneath parts of the house that I could take a screwdriver and punch large holes in them. The kitchen, at the very back of the house, was in such bad shape that it would have to be torn off. What I had thought solid wasn't solid at all.

Then the same afternoon, Kate came home, walked into the kitchen, and announced, "I quit my job today." The way she spoke I knew it was something she'd been planning. Without her working I would have to take out a bigger loan to pay for repairs on the house. And I would have to do more of the work myself. I couldn't believe what she had done.

Seth

I started working for Granddaddy after school was out. I'd walk up to the store every morning before he got there and work until one o'clock, pumping gas, stocking shelves, bagging groceries, and sometimes ringing up a sale if there weren't too many items. I'd worked some in the summers before, and it felt good to be doing it again. It was something I was used to, and everything else right about that time felt strange to me. Just when living with Grandmama and Granddaddy was beginning to seem normal, everything got changed.

One hot morning a couple of weeks after Daddy got married to Kate, I was walking to work and when I passed the graveyard I heard a gunshot back at our house, then heard someone yell. My heart started pounding and for a second I wasn't sure what to do, but I turned around and ran back to the house, and all kinds of ideas started coming into my mind. Daddy had already gone to work, and that left Kate and Erin there. Maybe Kate had picked up one of the .22 rifles or a pistol and accidentally made it go off. Maybe she'd shot herself by accident. Or maybe someone had tried to get in the house? Then I remembered that she'd been in Erin's room the night before and that they'd been arguing about something—they seemed to argue all the time—and a crazy idea came to me. Had Kate been arguing with Erin again and gotten so mad she'd shot her? That didn't seem possible, but for some reason I thought about it, if just for a second.

I ran up the steps and onto the porch, then called out Kate's name and said, "It's me." I didn't want her to think I was some stranger trying to break in. She didn't answer, and I used my key and went inside.

She wasn't in the hall or her bedroom or the living room, so I walked toward the back of the house and called her name again. She still didn't answer. I finally opened the heavy door to the kitchen and found the barrel of Daddy's .22 pistol pointed directly at my face. In the split second before I ducked, I saw a look of anger and fear in her squinted eyes. "Kate, it's me," I said. I felt like I'd broken into my own house.

"You scared the shit out of me!" she yelled.

She lowered the pistol, but her expression didn't change all that much. I walked into the kitchen, and the door, which wasn't plumb, shut behind me with a bang. The room was hot, like somebody had been cooking in it all night long. Kate had on a pink housecoat and her hair was a little wild. She kept staring at me as if she wasn't sure who I was.

"I'm sorry," I said, trying to get used to the fact that she'd just cussed me. No grown-up had ever done that. She didn't sound like a grown-up was supposed to sound. "I didn't mean to scare you. What happened?"

"I think some man was outside my bedroom window watching me get dressed." Her voice was shaky, like she was *still* ready to shoot someone.

"Did he try to come in? I heard a shot," I said.

"No. I shot through the window screen in the bedroom, at where I thought he was, out there in the yard where your father's been cutting down all that brush. I came back here to look out at the pasture, to see if he'd run this way."

What if I'd been outside? I thought. What if I'd walked to the

180

storage building behind the house for something before going to the store?

"I'll go look around," I said, glad to have thought of a way out of there.

Once in the yard, I didn't know what I ought to look for. It wasn't like anybody would still be around, and even though I knew you were supposed to trust grown-ups, something told me that no one had been outside. She'd only imagined it. Still, I searched in the bushes, looking for footprints or cigarette butts, like some television detective might. There wasn't anything, not that I could find.

When I went back inside, Kate's bedroom door was closed, but Erin opened hers. "What's going on?" she said. Her eyes were about half shut.

"Didn't you hear the gun go off?" I said.

"I heard something."

"And you're just now getting up?"

"What happened?" she said and motioned for me to come into her room.

"Your mother says she shot at someone."

She had her back to me and all she said was, "She's crazy." Then she climbed back in bed and sat up. A fan in a chair blew on her and she kept having to push her hair out of her face. "Damn, it's hot," she said.

"What do you mean by 'crazy'?"

"I doubt there was anybody out there. She's just scared living here because it isn't in some neighborhood with other houses all around. And she's probably still upset about us arguing last night."

"What were y'all arguing about?"

"I wanted to go spend the night in Demarville with my cousins, but she thinks all I wanted to do was stay out half the night and smoke dope."

What she said shocked me a little because she said it so easy, like she'd been talking about seeing her cousins and going to a movie or maybe to a church supper.

"Is that what you wanted to do?"

She smiled. "Yeah, but I sure didn't tell her that."

"Has she caught you before?"

"Yeah, but only once. We were still in Nashville, and some older guy gave me some, wanted me to try it, but I doubt that's all he wanted. Anyway, she found it. Now she's always asking if I'm still doing it."

"I wonder if she's told Daddy."

"I doubt it," she said. "Wouldn't want him to know just how wild her daughter is, not before they got married, at least." She laughed.

When I walked back past Kate's door, it was still shut, and I wondered what she was doing in there. Getting dressed? Worrying about Erin? Maybe she still felt scared. I hoped she'd put the gun down by now. When Daddy had told me they were going to get married, I don't think I ever expected her to feel like a mother to me, and now I knew she wouldn't. Besides, no one could replace my real mother, no matter how much I tried not to think about her or worry about her.

After I got to the store, Granddaddy put me to work cleaning out the back room. It was hotter in there than the kitchen had been. I didn't tell Granddaddy about what had happened. I'm not sure why. I mostly thought about what Erin had said. She stayed out late, doing all kinds of things probably, and she wasn't even as old as me. Nobody I knew did drugs, not around Riverfield, or at school. Then I remembered that there was somebody I knew who *did* do drugs, somebody who I hadn't seen in a long time. In some ways Erin reminded me of Michael, even though she was a girl and a lot younger, and it wasn't that I'd just found out she did drugs, either. The way she argued with her mother, the tough way she talked back to her, and just the way she looked and walked and wasn't afraid of adults, all those things made me think about my brother.

I not only hadn't seen Michael in over a year, I hadn't gotten a phone call or even a card. Maybe I didn't want to hear from him. It wasn't like he'd ever say he was sorry, and he'd only have been lying if he said he was. I wondered if Granddaddy had heard from him, or Mama. I doubted it. I felt like we were all pieces of something broken, like glass from an old jar or a chimney for a kerosene lamp like we sell in the store, broken into too many pieces to ever be repaired.

By the time I finished cleaning out the back room, after having to stop and pump gas or bag groceries or wipe sweat every few minutes, it was one o'clock. But I didn't really want to go home and be around Kate and Erin, and I didn't want to be by myself either. I guess I could have gone to see Carter, who lives just down the road, or Willie, who lives a little past him. They'd started getting friendlier at school, but they weren't who I wanted to see, not that day.

When I got to the house, instead of going in, I walked around to the side away from Kate's window and got my bike, then took off down the road. I didn't even stop to eat any lunch.

The shacks and cement block houses along the Loop Road didn't look any different than they had the last time I'd seen them. It seemed like the same people sat on their porches and front steps, fanning themselves, waiting for cars to pass.

I hadn't seen Bobby since school let out and hadn't been to his house in over a year. We were still friends, but only at school. I just hadn't wanted to go to his house, and he hadn't come to mine, not once. Maybe his mama wouldn't let him. Seemed like she'd decided she didn't like me anymore, but I hadn't done anything to her or anybody else. Sometimes you don't have to do anything for people not to like you. They blame you for things that really aren't your fault.

He was hoeing in the garden along with Johnny when I rode

up, and I hoped his mama wouldn't come out into the yard or the garden while I was there, but if she did, I'd just have to see her.

He looked up from his hoe and smiled at me when he heard my bike. "Hey stranger," he said. "We got another hoe that'll just fit your hands."

"All right," I said. "How much do you pay? A hundred dollars an hour?"

"You got it," he said. "At least when it's this hot."

I'd never worked in a garden before and was scared I wouldn't know what to do, but after Johnny went and got the hoe and Bobby showed me how to chop at the weeds, I stayed even with them, at least for a while. It felt like I'd just seen Bobby the day before the way he was so friendly.

"What you been up to?" Bobby said when we stopped at the end of a row.

"Working in Granddaddy's store, mostly."

"That's good. Make you a little money."

"Daddy got married," I said, but I figured he already knew.

"I heard."

"We moved in the old house near the church, and I've got a stepsister now."

"I heard that too. How old is she?" he said.

"Almost fourteen."

"She cute?"

"I guess so. I hadn't really thought about it that much."

"I hadn't been up that way in a long while. About time I made a trip, I reckon." He looked over at me and smiled again, like he was telling me he thought it was time things got back to normal for us.

"Come anytime," I said.

We went back to hoeing, and I thought that maybe we'd both decided right then that we didn't care anymore what our parents did or said or tried to keep us from doing.

After a while Bobby and Johnny got ahead of me. I couldn't

184

work the hoe as fast as they could, and blisters rose up on my hands.

"About time to quit," Bobby finally said. "Let's get us some water."

He'd probably quit sooner than he was supposed to, but we put our hoes up and got a drink from the hose at the back of the house.

"Want to walk out to the woods? Me and Johnny built a dam on the creek out there."

"Which way is it?" I said.

We started walking toward the line of trees and before long we were right in the middle of the sedge field where we'd flown kites that day with Frances. The sky was just as clear and the wind started to blow hard. I wondered if Bobby was thinking about that day with the kites, and if maybe he was thinking about Frances too.

She must have had her baby before Christmas. Bobby had never said anything about it, and maybe that meant he didn't know. I'd never told him. I'd learned how not to talk about something, and maybe Bobby had too, though I hoped not. I wondered if Frances had kept the baby. I could see her as a mama, holding the baby, playing with it, letting it pull on her blond hair. I missed her a lot when I'd picture her that way, and I'd wonder if she ever thought about me, but her mind was probably on her baby, even if she had given it away. Maybe especially if she'd given it away.

We walked on through the sedge, and the hot wind blew in gusts and brought up the sharp smell of the dried stalks like some kind of fine powder you could light with a match and that would burn in the air. The sweat rolled off my face, and my shirt stuck to my shoulders and back and pulled at me.

We finally made the woods and got to the creek. They'd used pieces of tin and some posts to make the dam, and the water had risen to the top of the tin and ran clear over its rusty edges. The clay banks were shady and steep, and the water had crept up high enough so that you could swim and not just wade.

"Better than taking a bath," Bobby said and took off his shirt. Johnny already had his underwear hanging on a limb.

I hesitated a little.

"Ain't no girls out here," Bobby said. "Come on."

I thought again about Frances and took my clothes off. Both of them jumped in and yelled when they came back up for air, and then I jumped. We splashed Johnny and swam for a little while. The water felt cool and took the heat out of me that had felt like a fever since that morning.

We ended up standing at the dam where the water ran a little faster and colder against our chests.

"Beats hoeing a garden, don't it?" Bobby smiled.

"Or cleaning out a hot storage room," I said.

Sunlight broke through a place in the trees then and reflected off the water in bright streaks, and a woodpecker started pecking somewhere above us in a big oak.

"Reckon Mama's home yet and sees we ain't finished the garden?" Johnny said.

"Maybe so." Bobby splashed the water with the palm of his hand. "We can finish it tomorrow."

"She might be mad, though. Might get Daddy after us."

"It'll wait till tomorrow. Let them get mad if they want."

"Grown-ups are fucking crazy as shit," I said suddenly, without even realizing I was going to say it, or that I was going to cuss.

Bobby looked at me a little funny for a second, like he had some serious questions he wanted to ask me, questions he thought I might have the answers to. "They sure are," he said finally, and that was all he said.

At the supper table that night I sat there with Daddy and Kate and Erin and when Daddy asked what I'd been doing with myself that day, I just shrugged and told him I rode my bike around and didn't tell him I'd seen Bobby. He didn't need to know everything I did.

Then Kate looked at me a little hard, waiting, it seemed, to hear what else I might say. But I didn't tell anything, and she didn't either. Maybe she had decided she'd overreacted, or that there hadn't been anybody out there that morning after all. But it could have been that she was just afraid that if she told about shooting through the screen, the other part would have to come out too, about how she'd pointed the gun at me, maybe even come close to pulling the trigger right there in the room where we sat.

Erin kept watching all three of us, smiling a little every once in a while, like we were putting on a show for her and she already knew how it would end. I wondered what she knew, if her mother had told *her* about pointing the gun at me. I couldn't tell. It was like she was separated from us, watching from the other side of a window. Then I wondered if she'd been smoking dope somewhere down in the pasture and was high.

Daddy started to talk to Kate about doing some more work on the house, but she wasn't really listening, and neither was I. Kate looked far away. Maybe she was thinking again about that morning, or only that she'd better not tell what she'd done. Then I heard Daddy say my name, and suddenly I felt like I was looking through a window too, that all of us were. We were all on ladders outside the kitchen looking in at ourselves and at each other.

Laura

My father told me that Conrad had gotten married again. I wasn't surprised to hear it. I had dated some, though not seriously. Perhaps I didn't want to get too close to a man, didn't want to lose any control over my life. Since the divorce I'd gotten a job in marketing for a medical supply company. I had more responsibility than at any other job I'd ever had, and it felt good. I'd traveled some, too, on money that my father had given me. I went to New England with a friend one fall, and to the Blue Ridge mountains in late summer.

So marrying again wasn't anything I wanted, but I knew that it was something Conrad would want. What surprised me wasn't his remarrying, but my hearing from his new wife, a woman I had never met.

She called late on a Saturday morning. I knew that Conrad must have been out of the house. Maybe Seth too. She told me who she was and tried to explain in an anxious voice why she'd called, but she didn't explain it very well. "He takes long walks," she finally said.

"Who?"

"Conrad," she said. "He goes off down in the pasture for hours sometimes. I don't know why. He just disappears."

"That sounds like him," I said, really thinking, though, that taking a walk isn't that out of the ordinary for someone like Conrad who grew up out in the country, but she probably felt excluded.

"He's out walking right now. He's been gone almost an hour."

"Is Seth with him?"

"No. Seth's up at the store," she said, which surprised me, the fact that he wasn't with his father.

"How is he?"

"Seth's fine," she said. "He's working part-time for his grandfather."

When she spoke Seth's name I felt a little sick in my stomach. It was as if she had taken my place, knew more about my son than I did, and I envied her. I wondered then if Seth might even call her "Mama," and the thought made me hurt. Her voice sounded so flat when she spoke about him, and she didn't say anything complimentary, which made me wonder if they got along. I almost hoped they didn't, and then found myself wanting to hang up.

"Conrad's mother is a bitch," she said. It appeared that May had been hinting that she get another job. Maybe more than hinting. She told me that she had quit her old one not long after she'd married Conrad. She said that she didn't feel as if she ought to work. She wanted sympathy more than advice, and finally I had neither for her, but I was polite.

She eventually hung up, and all I could think was, At least I worked. May had to give me that. Maybe she would see that I hadn't been so bad a wife and mother after all, and I could only wonder why this new wife deserved to be with Seth when I couldn't even *see* him.

I thought of Seth often, worried about him. Sometimes I'd imagine what he might be doing the very moment he crossed my mind. I'd wonder if he had made many friends, if he had a girlfriend, and I'd wonder what he looked like, what kind of man he was becoming. Was his hair growing darker? Was he filling out?

189

And did he know how to be decent to others, a compassionate and forgiving person?

It had been comforting to know exactly where he was when I talked to the new wife, but upsetting too, because I knew that I couldn't go to the store and see him, could not set foot there. I felt as if I were losing years of his life. And mine, too.

But at least Seth was safe from harm, that was reasonably certain, especially with Conrad as a father. For Michael, nothing was certain. Except for a cryptic postcard from Fort Walton Beach, I hadn't heard a word from him in over a year. All the card said was, "Having a wonderful time listening to the ocean tell my fortune. Only good things come out of the water and the earth." What is one to make of that? I didn't know if he was on a tug, or working at all; and I worried that he might be doing something illegal, or taking hard drugs, or both. More and more I expected a phone call from some policeman telling me my son was dead. And I didn't even know where the call might come from. Was he living in Fort Walton, or anywhere in the state of Florida?

My father had told me how Michael had left Valhia suddenly, without saying good-bye, and he'd told me why; but to imagine Michael a father, even in the loosest sense of the word, and myself a grandmother to a child I would probably never see, was almost beyond me. It all seemed so far removed from the life I had come to live, a life completely separate from husband, children, and parents, everyone who had helped to define what my life was and who I was. Whenever I thought of *family*, all I could see was a photograph of myself with the faces and bodies of people around me faded and blurred by exposure to a light bright enough to burn.

I knew the parents of the girl Michael had been with, but not well. Her father, James, had been a year or two ahead of Conrad in school, and his sister, Jean, had been much younger. Conrad had dated her when he first got out of the service, before we began to date. It might have gotten serious, but she broke it off for whatever reason. Maybe the age difference. Conrad didn't talk about it. There had been a rumor once that James's child was really his sister's, that he and his wife had taken it to raise as their own, and it may have been true. There had been another rumor too, that Conrad was the child's father; but I'd asked him before we married, and he'd said no, that it couldn't be his. If it had been, I believed he would have told me. I'd had no question of that. He was an honorable man and I knew the way rumors spread in small towns among women who don't have to work and who have no better way to occupy their time than to look for the worst in others instead of in themselves.

But after talking with my father and thinking about the rumor again, I wasn't so sure. If the rumor had been true, it meant that Conrad had kept a secret from me, had lied, something I hadn't thought him capable of, and it also meant that we now shared a grandchild the same way we shared a child, across a great divide of hurts and mistakes.

Lies and families can become such tangled things.

Michael

Traveling Man. That's what you might have called me. Not a bad way to make a living, but not as good as being out on a tug with the salt sticking to your skin and the ocean whispering her secrets in your ear like some woman telling you just where to touch her, but better than loading trucks, and damn sure better than sitting at a desk.

Of course, my traveling, my endeavor into the world of commerce and shipping, eventually came to an end, a sudden end, though I really can't say I didn't see it coming. But that was later, after I'd learned the backroads and the little two-redlight one-horse towns of South Alabama and the Florida panhandle, learned them like a tug master learns the shipping lanes and the whorehouses by the docks.

When I left Valhia in the old El Camino, with not much more than my duffel bag and some hard muscles in my arms from loading all those trucks, I headed straight down to Fort Walton Beach, out of trouble and into the land of water and sun and women, and maybe opportunity, and got in touch with a man who had business connections of a certain type. I had his number, and a reference, you might say, from the loading dock, a fine fellow who had information of a kind you don't get in school. Let's just say he'd spent a little time in a state-run institution, and was now retired from his former career but still had connections of his own.

I made Fort Walton, met the man who shall remain nameless, and learned how to handle our product. They taught me how to weigh and count those imported bricks and how to store them away for shipping, and I learned destinations and travel routes. It wasn't the big time, no major corporation, but a thriving little business all the same, with no worry about tax laws.

Every once in a while I got to go out on the water at night. I'd farm myself out, do a little side work with a bigger company, and pick up some quick extra money. But it was more dangerous. We'd run with no lights and cut through the dark and the waves beneath a quarter moon, maybe a few stars. Then we'd see a small flash of light and rendezvous with another boat and transfer cargo. We'd work fast and quiet, nothing but shadows on the water. I'd feel like some ghost of a pirate from early times, riding in a wooden ship, a regular sea dog, not bound to anything or anyone or any place.

By June I'd been at it for a little more than a year, and long since sold the El Camino. I'd bought a brand new four-door Chevrolet. Didn't want anything that called too much attention to itself, but it had an air conditioner that would freeze you to the seat and a stereo that would pin your ears back. I had a nice little place in Fort Walton, too.

At the end of that hot-ass month of June, when I was thanking the Lord for my air conditioner on a run to Bayou la Batre, I stopped outside of Gulf Shores at a fine little establishment called the Flora-Bama feeling mighty dry and dusty inside. You could say it was a dry and dusty time in a lot of ways. For one thing, too many people were of the opinion that I owed them money. Not business associates, just the landlord and the people down at the power company, even the phone company was threatening. Maybe I'd been living a little beyond my means. But I knew I'd be all right. I still had some cash.

So I sat there in the bar with one leg on each side of the dividing line and got drunk in two states at once, good and drunk, double drunk, enough to make me walk out to the ocean and listen to the waves. The tide was coming in and the wind was blowing so slow and easy. It was the kind of night when you *ought* to feel like all is right with the world.

I decided I'd put myself to sleep and spend the night under the stars and in the dunes, so I walked up the beach to a liquor store and bought a pint of rum. Then I went back to the spot I'd found, leaned back on a piece of driftwood, and sipped slow and watched the waves and let them tell me bedtime stories about wine and women and sea dogs of old.

But I couldn't sleep, and the good stories stopped coming. Later on the wind picked up and the waves grew and crashed louder. Then the rum started running around in my head and the stories came back, only they weren't good stories, not now. They were stories that I already knew and didn't want to hear anymore, stories that had been sounding in my head for a year or more, and that I couldn't shake or bring to a "The End." You could say they were about fathers who don't care about sons and brothers who are favored and daughters long forgotten. Yeah, that's what they were about. Regular fairy tales without the "happily ever after."

There stood my father, wearing his sunglasses, selling beer, and flirting with the women who come in his place, women with big hair, some of them young, or young enough, all with rough hard voices. I heard them in my head just as clear as a bell ringing on a buoy and twice as loud. *You got any handsome sons?* a woman said. I heard her right there where I sat. You better believe it. *Maybe one who looks like you? No*, my father told her. *No kids. At least none that I know about.* She laughed, but he laughed harder. *You sure you ain't got any kids? A man like you?* another woman said. *Well, not any I'd want to claim.* They all laughed, loud enough for me to hear it over the crash of the waves, just like I was listening from a corner booth.

Then Seth sat there at the edge of the water, the wind blowing his hair, looking all spoiled, the perfect son. He got claimed. The only one who did. Frances sure as hell didn't, not till I came along. You can say I laid claim to her all right, and left the proof behind. Flesh of my flesh and bone of my bone, like a preacher would say, one who might be trying to save me, or make me do the "right thing." But I did what I wanted and I wanted Frances, wanted to claim her in a way that would leave its mark, or my mark, forever.

But maybe she laid a claim on me, too, one that I didn't even know about, couldn't have known about, until the next time I was with a woman. It was a redhead I met in a Fort Walton bar. I took her home, but I started thinking about Frances, about that night in the shack, and the nights after that, and finally when Frances told me she was pregnant. We'd been sitting in the truck by the river, and she was surprised that I *wasn't* surprised, but even though I'd been waiting on it, way down inside it was like I *couldn't* believe it, like it was a surprise that it could happen and did happen. Then after that scene with my brother at the loading dock, I was gone. And there I was in that redhead's arms, and all I could goddamn think about was Frances and the baby and my father and Conrad and what I'd done, and that redhead wanted to know what was the matter. Was she doing something wrong? It's all right. Just tell her what to do, she said. It happens. Come on, baby. Let me help you. Relax. Tell me what to do. I said, "Just leave." And the next time was the same, too. Nothing but what I'd done in my mind, almost like I'd killed somebody. What am I doing wrong? the girl said, just like the one before, beautiful and naked. Tell me what to do. It'll be okay. Relax. "Just leave," I said again, and knew then that it was going to be bad, a dry and dusty time. But for how long? What had happened to me? Had I become less than a man?

195

Those waves kept crashing in the wind and somebody started laughing somewhere out on the dunes, and the wind carried it, whipped it around until I couldn't tell where it was coming from, like it came from everywhere and nowhere, or maybe it was only coming out of my own mind, or maybe my own mouth. Maybe I was laughing at my own drunk, dead self.

Then there was nothing at all, except a thin line of light on the edge of the ocean, the beginning of morning, and a hard sudden pain in my head, then another, and the only light I could see after that was right behind my eyes, a bright light that faded and pulsed. Then another pain, in my side this time, and there was laughing in my ear. "Hit the motherfucker again," I heard, and all I could think was Jesus, God. Oh, Jesus. Then hands were rolling me over.

When I came to, a crowd was staring at me, and a little girl in a red bathing suit said, "Look at that man, Mama. What's wrong with him?" I made myself stand up, then spit blood.

My keys were in my pocket, which meant that I still had my car, and hopefully all that was in it, but my money was gone, and I didn't know exactly how much, but enough. Almost all the money that I'd had left in the world. The only thing I knew for sure then was that I'd just gone from dry and dusty times straight into nothing but hard times.

Conrad

Erin was, in many ways, a female version of Michael. Her room always smelled of cigarettes, and she was usually withdrawn and aloof in a way you would not expect from a girl her age. Or perhaps that is the way girls her age had begun to act. I tried to get to know her, but she went to Demarville so often and usually stayed in town until late into the evening. At the supper table—when she was home for supper—she would barely answer her mother's questions about her day, let alone mine. It was at those moments, when I suspect she was under the influence of marijuana, that she most reminded me of Michael and made me wonder if she were already beyond reach, as he was and had been for so long. I tried to talk to Kate about making Erin stay home more and giving her chores to do, responsibilities, but she said she'd decided that Erin needed to be with friends, girls her age, that she would grow out of this "stage" she was going through if we left her alone and didn't antagonize her. All I knew was that Michael had never grown out of it.

But it wasn't just Michael who Erin put me in mind of. When she was in the living room looking at a woman's fashion magazine, or sat out in the swing on the front porch painting her fingernails, or was perhaps asking her mother about getting her ears pierced, I could not help but think of Frances, of what it might have been like to have had my daughter to raise for all those years; and I would feel then a sense of loss for something I had never really known, and could only be thankful that Frances, because of her ignorance, didn't have to suffer any kind of similar loss. She had a family that loved her and that she knew as her own and was just as confident in that knowledge as any other child would have been.

And if I had ever seriously considered interfering, the letter I received from Jean made me put aside such selfish thoughts.

James must have told her where I worked, and she probably sent the letter there rather than to the house so that I would not have to explain to anyone what it was or who it was from. She told me that Frances had been living with her, and that once Frances went off to school, she and her husband would raise the child, but that the child, whose name was Julia, would know who its real mother was as soon as it was old enough to understand. "I do not expect, nor want, any financial support from the father," she went on to say, "but I would appreciate your continued support while Frances is in college." She told me that I could send the money directly to her now. Her tone was very business-like, and then she softened a bit and said that she hoped I was doing well and that if I had ever entertained any notions of telling Frances that I was her father, to please not give in to them. "I have come close to telling her the truth many times since she has been with me, but have decided that it is far too late at this point. Sometimes secrets have to be kept. There is no going back and making choices over again." She then asked me to destroy the letter, and as I tore it into pieces, I realized that her request to remain silent exempted me from ever having to take responsibility for my daughter, and this, though it may seem odd, was not a relief.

The same day I received the letter, I had to go home and work on replacing one of the joists beneath the house. Physical work has a way of clearing my mind, and it helped me to not think about Jean or Frances. I had taken my father's truck a few days before, gone to the sawmill in Demarville, and had them load up the heavy seven-foot oak piece. Now it had to be put into place. I'd rented a couple of railroad jacks, and with the help of Seth and two black men, Henry and Big Man, who I'd managed to catch up at the store, we lifted the house with the jacks just enough to pull out the old rotten piece, and then the four of us picked up the new joist and after a great deal of sweating and straining, pushed it into place. I then took a sledge hammer and finished driving it home.

Seth was more help lifting it than I thought he would be. He'd gotten so much stronger, and as he'd pushed and shoved he seemed to be acting out of anger, almost. I had to recognize that he was getting older as he stood sweating and dirty beside Henry and Big Man. He wasn't as tall as either of them, but he was certainly as tall as some men, if not as filled out yet.

"We need to go ahead and load up the old joist so we can haul it off," I said, a little anxious about Seth's reaction to doing more work. Often, as we'd begun to do work on the house together, he was impatient with me. The week before, when I'd asked him to help me repair the roof on the old pumphouse, he'd done the work but had said very little. I suppose he'd had things he would rather have been doing, or perhaps a son always reaches that point when he doesn't want to be around his father, when he reacts with dissidence at any suggestion or request a father makes.

After we loaded the old joist, I paid Henry and Big Man ten dollars each and took them back up to the store. Then Seth and I drove into the pasture and pushed the old rotten piece of the house off the tailgate and down into a gravel pit that had been dug when I was a boy.

"Did slaves make that?" he said.

At first I thought he meant the pit, but then realized that he was talking about the old joist.

"Yes," I said. "I'm sure they did. Hand hewn with axes. It's amazing how straight and smooth they could make them, almost as if they had done the cutting with a blade. It's craftsmanship that you'd never find now."

"How long do you think it will take us to get the house all fixed?"

"I don't know exactly," I said. "It may take awhile, and the house will look a little different, but it will get done. That's a promise."

For a moment, as we stood at the edge of that pit, I put my hand on his shoulder and I could see all the rotten sills and joists replaced, the house freshly painted, and even the old garden replanted.

At supper that night it was just the three of us. Erin had stayed in town, of course, and Kate had spent the day stripping the large French doors between the living room and what used to be Grandmother's room. They looked good, and she said that they would look even better after she put on a coat of varnish. Since she had quit her job, she'd been doing more work around the house than I'd expected of her.

After supper we went out on the porch and talked while twilight turned to dark and the lightning bugs came out. Kate and I rocked back and forth in the swing and Seth sat at the top of the steps, and as it grew darker, as the shadows faded, the darkness seemed to take us not just into night, but back into time, to another place almost.

"This is the way we used to spend summer evenings when I was a child," I said.

"We did, too," Kate said. "It would be so hot inside that you didn't want to go in until you had to, and you could look up and down the street we lived on and see other families on their porches. It was a different time. It must sound like the Middle Ages to kids like Seth."

"No television," I said.

"We did have radio, though."

"Yes, and we'd listen to war news when my father got home from the store, and I loved 'The Lone Ranger.'"

"Seth, can you imagine life without television?" Kate said.

"Sometimes," he said. "Since we've been living here, anyway."

"But you don't want us to sell our set, do you?" she said.

"No." He laughed a little. "I wouldn't want to do anything like that."

Finally the stars began to come out, and while we sat quietly looking at the night sky, I remembered again the sound of my grandmother's voice, the sight of my father pulling into the yard, and the smell of the kitchen when Leathy Ann cooked; and then I looked at Seth and Kate and thought about the work we'd done on the house, what we'd managed so far, and I began to feel again a rediscovery of something lost but that maybe *could* be realized once again, made tangible.

Then I recalled the letter I'd received that morning and knew that not all things can be regained.

One afternoon, toward the end of the week, something unexpected happen, and yet it's odd how events seem to occur when they should, as if everything has been pointing toward a particular moment. Kate had called me at work and asked me to pick up Erin before I came home. I went by the cleaners first, and as I got out of my car, I heard a feminine voice call "Mr. Anderson," and for some reason, even though I had never really spoken to her before, I knew instinctively who it was. Or maybe it wasn't instinct at all, maybe it was because I'd had her on my mind all week and the soft voice I heard merely brought her back to mind, but there Frances was walking toward me, looking so much like her mother.

"How is Seth?" she said, as if we had spoken of him before.

"He's fine," I told her.

She pulled back her blond hair and looked about a bit nervously, but not really any more so than some other teenager might who was having to speak to an adult she really didn't know.

"I'd like to see him," she said. "It's been awhile. I've been living over in Mississippi."

"I'm sure he'd like to see you, too. Are you home for long?"

"Only a few days," she said and then pursed her lips together tightly, as if she might say more but wasn't sure if she should. She looked toward the traffic a moment and pulled at her hair again. "Well, it was nice to see you."

"It was nice to see you, too," I said.

She walked toward her car then, and it struck me as she waved good-bye and drove away that our conversation had been so casual. I don't know what I had expected, some dramatic moment perhaps. But she'd appeared so unexpectedly that I hadn't had time to become nervous or over anxious, and for a moment longer I just stood there, probably looking foolish to anyone passing, and said to myself over and over, That was your daughter you just talked to.

Seth

I'd just gotten off work at the store and was walking home past the church and the graveyard when I heard either a car or a truck with bad brakes slowing down behind me. I didn't turn around and look, but only stepped farther away from the road, figuring somebody was probably fixing to blow their horn. Then I saw the hood of a blue truck right beside me and knew.

"Don't you ever watch for traffic?" Frances said through the open window.

I smiled at her and she stopped in the road.

"Well quit grinning and get in before something hits us," she said.

I climbed in the cab and pushed a toolbox out from under my feet, then retied the strings on my tennis shoes even though they weren't all that loose. For some reason I felt a little shy with her.

"I almost didn't recognize you," she said. "You're getting to be tall, like your daddy, and your hair's a little darker. At first I thought, Who's that man up there?" She laughed.

"Daddy told me you were home," I said.

"Have you eaten lunch?"

"Not yet."

"Well I'm taking you to Demarville for a hamburger."

She drove on past the house. Erin sat out on the porch

painting her toenails it looked like and didn't see me go by in the truck. She didn't even look up.

"Was that your stepsister?" Frances said after a minute or so.

"Yes."

"So how do you like having a sister?"

"Well, she doesn't feel like a sister, not a real one, anyway. It's like she's some cousin I've just met. But we get along all right, I guess."

She turned onto the highway and picked up speed. The grass along the road had just been cut by the county, and the wind in the cab had that fresh sweet smell to it.

She'd said that I looked different, and as she leaned over the steering wheel and stared past the cracks in the windshield I tried to see if she'd changed any. Her hair was longer, and she might have gained a little weight, but other than that, she looked the same. I don't know what I thought. Just because she'd had a baby didn't mean that she was going to look like a different person, even if she was changed inside in the way she felt about herself. Besides, she'd always looked to me like she was grown, like she could sit with grown-up mothers and not look out of place. She still looked like that.

But then all of a sudden Michael came to mind and I couldn't help but think of the two of them together, that she hadn't had just *a* baby, but Michael's baby, that he'd taken her off somewhere—maybe to a hotel room. Then I noticed she was wearing white shorts and that her legs were brown and long and smooth and that the shorts fit her a little tight, or maybe it was just because of the way she sat, but she looked good in them and I didn't want to stop looking. I'd always thought she was pretty, but now she was something more than pretty. So maybe she did look different from the last time I'd seen her, or maybe it was that I was different, changed in some way besides being taller.

We ate at a place right beside the Tennahpush River. Both of us had hamburgers. She'd told me on the way to town that she was going off to school in the fall, and I wondered what she had done with the baby, if she had put it up for adoption, or if maybe something bad had happened to it. I knew babies died sometimes. I wanted to ask her while we sat there eating, but she was talking about Bobby and about how their parents expected him to work more than he should have to, Johnny too, and I didn't want to interrupt her and didn't really know, anyway, if I should ask her about the baby or not.

"What's wrong?" I heard her say finally, like she was reading my mind again.

"What? Nothing."

"Tell me," she said. "I can see in your face that something's bothering you. You can't fool me."

"I know you had a baby," I said. I couldn't not say it. It just came out. "And I know who the father is."

"It's a girl," she said without acting surprised, like she'd been waiting on me to say something. "Her name's Julia. Julia Elizabeth."

"Is she all right?"

"She's beautiful."

"Where is she?" I said.

"With my aunt in Mississippi. I'm going back tomorrow. This is my first time away from her and I miss her."

"Why didn't you bring her with you?"

"My parents don't want people to know. They made me go live with my aunt while I was pregnant. I told them it was stupid, that I didn't care if people knew. It's not like this is the 50's still, I said. But they wouldn't listen. I don't care if you tell people or not. It's okay if you do."

"Does Bobby know?"

"I told him on the phone before I had her. He knew something was wrong when I left, and I didn't want him not to know. You worry more when you don't know what's going on, no matter how bad it might be. Not knowing's worse. Bobby didn't tell you?"

"No."

"Who did?"

"Michael," I said.

She seemed surprised. "Do you see him? Is he around?"

"No. He's gone. Said he was going to Florida. He told me right before he left town and I haven't heard from him since. He just ran off."

"I'm sorry you don't see him. Maybe it's better that you don't. I know I don't want to see him."

"I'm sorry," I said.

"For what?"

"For what he did to you. How he treated you."

"You don't have to apologize for your brother, Seth. Besides, it's my fault too."

"What about when you go off to school?"

"You mean the baby?"

"Yes."

"My aunt's going to keep her. I'll see her most weekends, and when I'm finished, she'll go with me wherever I get a job. My aunt told me I just *had* to go to college. She said she wouldn't hear of anything else. My parents wanted me to give her up for adoption, but Aunt Jean told me I didn't have to, that I could make my own decision. She's been so good to me."

Frances was quiet then and ate the last few bites of her hamburger. I'd been finished. She wiped her mouth with a napkin and took out a mirror and some lipstick from her purse, and I watched as she spread the lipstick. It was a dark reddish color and I saw how full her lips were and thought again about her long smooth legs and how she looked in her white shorts. Then I tried to think about something else.

When I started to get up she told me to wait a minute.

"What is it?" I said.

"I just wanted to ask you about something." She closed her purse and looked at me like she wasn't sure if she should say what she was thinking.

"What?" I said.

"Your mother. Have you seen or heard from her?"

"No," I said and suddenly felt tight inside, like a hand was squeezing me.

"Do you miss her?"

"Yes," I said. I couldn't help but feel like I was admitting something I shouldn't, though, something terrible.

"Do you ever think about seeing her?"

"Not really. I just try *not* to think about her."

"But that doesn't work, does it?"

I felt again like she was seeing into me, like she hadn't been gone all that time and still knew me just as well as ever. "No," I said and looked down at the table. "It doesn't work."

"I didn't mean to make you sad. Don't worry. You'll see your mother again. I don't know when, but you will. And try not to be too mad at your father."

"Are you ready to go?" I said, and that was all.

Later, when she pulled into our driveway, Erin was gone from the porch and Kate's car wasn't there. I figured they'd driven into town.

"Give me a hug, Seth," Frances said then.

And so I reached across the seat and let her put her arms around me and she hugged me tight, and all of a sudden I wanted to cry. Maybe it was because I knew I wouldn't see her again for a long time, or maybe it was because she'd made me think about my mother, made me miss her more than ever.

I finally pulled away from her and slid toward the door.

"Take care of yourself," she said. "And tell your daddy I said hello."

"I will," I said and that was all I could get out. I climbed from the truck and walked toward the house, but as soon as she pulled away I turned and headed for the pasture and the creek, wanting just to walk beside the muddy water beneath the shade of the oaks and sycamores and sweet gums and not think about anything at all.

That evening at supper all four of us were home. Kate fixed hamburgers and we ate out on the back porch while Daddy talked about how he used to play with his electric train when he was little in the spot where we sat, and how his great-grandfather, Grandpa Wilkie, who lived with them then, would blow pipe smoke into the engine and they would watch as it came out of the smoke stack. "That was just after we got electricity," he said, and Erin was about shocked to hear that the house hadn't always had electricity.

One of Erin's cousins came and picked her up later and took her to Demarville, and Daddy and Kate and I sat in the living room where two fans were blowing and played gin, something we'd never done before. It was Kate's idea, and she taught me how to play. Daddy usually wasn't much for playing cards, but it seemed like he thought it was a good idea, and before long he was winning most of the games.

"I think maybe I need some better competition," he said after a while. "A little bit of a challenge."

"You just wait," Kate said. "I'm going to beat you this time."

"I can't imagine what would make you think such a thing. You must be suffering from delusions or something," he said, laughing, teasing her in a way that I hadn't heard before.

"Looks like you're the one suffering from delusions," she said. "Delusions of grandeur."

She did win the next game, and I finally won one. Not long after, she said she was getting tired and went into their bedroom. Daddy and I put away the card table and the chairs we'd brought up from the kitchen. Then he said he thought he might go on to bed too, that he was a little tired, and I realized that maybe he just wanted to be alone with her.

I went out on the back porch again and watched lightning bugs and listened to the quiet of the night. Kate seemed easier to be with and she and Daddy were getting along. As I sat there in the dark, I decided that maybe Daddy was happy for the first time in a long time, or at least that he was beginning to feel some kind of happiness, and it was because of Kate, or seemed to be. Maybe they were learning how to live together, and maybe Kate was different from what I'd thought she was—not so crazy after all. It just takes people awhile to learn how to live together, I thought, and maybe everybody has the right to act a little crazy sometimes, even mothers.

Something Frances had said earlier that day came back to me like a whisper then, like she'd had a reason for saying it that she couldn't have known. "Don't worry. You'll see your mother again," she'd said, and it seemed possible suddenly. I felt like maybe before long it would be all right to tell Daddy that I wanted to see her, that he would be ready to hear it soon, and that somehow Kate was the reason he would be ready. For two years I'd tried not to think about Mama, felt like I couldn't, or shouldn't, but now that Daddy had gotten married, things were changed in a way that I'd never thought they would be. Daddy had someone else.

So there I sat in the dark while it kept getting later and later. Only a few lightning bugs flashed still. It felt more than peaceful out. Then I thought about Mama and what she might be doing. I imagined that she would most likely tell me it was time to go to bed if she knew that I was still awake. I wished that she could know I was thinking about her, that I'd never really stopped, as hard as I'd tried.

Late that night, very late, after I'd finally gone to sleep, I woke up and saw shadows against shadows on my walls and heard some kind of a commotion in Erin's room, like someone had fallen on the floor hard enough to hurt themselves. Then there was the sound of two voices, arguing, getting louder and louder.

"You're drunk!" Kate yelled. Eventually their voices faded, or maybe I just went back to sleep, not wanting to hear anything else, or to think about what might be happening.

The next morning there was a commotion in my room.

The sound of footsteps pounding down the back porch was what woke me up. Then I heard a fist beating on my door like somebody was trapped on the other side. At first I was afraid that someone, Daddy maybe, had been hurt, that he needed to be rushed to the hospital. I sat up in bed and before I could say anything, Kate burst in. The door hadn't been locked.

Her eyes were squinted and she stood there shaking. She looked the same as when she'd pointed the pistol at me—angry and scared. "Goddamnit, where is my gold watch?" she said.

I was still half asleep and wasn't really sure why she thought I could answer her. "What watch?" I said.

"The one you took out of my jewelry box. What did you do with it?"

I didn't say anything, just sat there with my mouth open, beginning to understand what was happening.

"Did you think you were going to sell it, or did you take it out of pure meanness? Do you even know why you took it?"

"I didn't take it," I said, hardly able to make the words come out of my mouth because I knew that she wouldn't believe anything I said.

"Of course you took it. You don't fool me. You never have. You're not the *good* boy your daddy thinks you are."

Then suddenly I saw Daddy standing in the door behind her. I don't know how long he'd been there. "What in the world do you think you're doing, Kate?" he said. He looked more surprised and shocked than mad, like he was looking at the back of a crazy person.

"All I know is, my watch is missing," she said, but even though she was answering him, she kept staring at me, like that *wasn't* all she knew.

Finally she turned around and walked past Daddy and back out onto the porch. Her footsteps were just as hard then as before.

Daddy sat down next to me on the bed. "I don't know what's gotten into her, but I'm going to find out," he said. Now he was definitely mad. "Are you all right?"

I nodded my head. For some reason though, I felt guilty, but I didn't know what for. Kate had been so hateful and mad that I couldn't help but think that something must be my fault, like maybe I had taken the watch, and forgotten.

"I know you didn't steal anything. You would never do that," Daddy said. "Let me go talk to her." He got up. "It'll be all right."

But I knew it wouldn't be.

Kate came back about fifteen minutes later, by herself, and stood over my bed. She wouldn't look at me, though, only at the floor. "I'm sorry," she said. "I shouldn't have accused you. I was wrong." Then she glanced up at me. Her face was pinched, her eyes squinted again, like she was sighting down a gun barrel. She caught my eyes for a second before she turned to leave, but the glance was long enough for me to know that all she'd said was a lie. And she'd wanted me to know it.

May

Conrad left for the store a little early on Monday morning. He had to get an order ready for a salesman. So when Seth wasn't sitting on a bench out front waiting for him to open, like usual, he wasn't surprised. But after he'd been open half an hour and Seth still hadn't shown up, he knew something was wrong. First he called Kate to see if maybe Seth had overslept. She told him that he'd left for work like normal, as far as she knew, but she checked his room anyway and said he wasn't there. Conrad told me she sounded funny, though, like she knew *something* must be wrong.

He called me just after that, to see if Seth had come over from across the pasture. I was worried right away, but Conrad said for me to come up to the store and that he'd go look for him, that he was probably just down along the creek or at the railroad trestle, some place where boys naturally have to go. But I don't think he really believed what he said.

When he came back around lunchtime and didn't have Seth with him, I'm the one who finally called Son and told him we didn't know where Seth was. It was a hard call, but I had to go ahead and let Son know what was going on.

He got to the store about one o'clock and had already checked the woods at the back of the graveyard and the old family plot. He said Seth liked to go there sometimes.

From the phone in the store, he called down to Bobby's house. I'd made a few calls already but hadn't tried there. I'd thought about it, but hadn't. Bobby happened to answer the phone and told Son that he hadn't seen Seth. I didn't figure Seth had gone down there. It would have been far too long a walk, and Kate had called much earlier and told me his bike was still at the house. When Kate called she didn't volunteer to help look or offer any suggestions about where he might be, which seemed strange to me.

"I'm going to look down in the pasture," Son said after a few minutes.

"I looked there a good bit," Conrad said, "but maybe he just didn't want to answer when I called out."

"That's what I'm thinking," Son said. "I'm going to walk the whole creek and check the far corner, too. Maybe you could go check back around the cribs."

So they left and I stayed in the store. There weren't many customers, but when one came in who I knew, which was just about all who did come in, I asked if they'd seen Seth. None of them had. It was like he'd left the house, walked down the steps, and disappeared before he'd passed through the front gate.

I started to worry more and more about things I didn't want to think about, things like you hear about on the news that are only supposed to happen in big cities up North. I even turned on the radio to see if there were any escaped convicts in the countryside, which has happened a few times over the years. They escape off the work farm near Selma. But there wasn't any news like that. Between customers, I'd pray. First that he was all right, then that we'd find him soon.

By the time Son and Conrad came back it was near closing and I was worried sick. They had both driven in different directions on the highway, one toward Valhia, the other toward Demarville. Then they'd started around the Loop Road from different points and met each other without seeing him.

They'd asked along the way if anyone had seen him, and they'd both stopped at the Bait Shop after trying the Loop Road, but nobody had seen him there, either.

So I called the sheriff before we left the store, and he said that if Seth hadn't gotten home by that night, to call him back. I was more than a little put out with him when he wouldn't do anything right away.

Conrad and I locked up the store, and Son went down to The Landing to check there one more time. His daddy had told him that he'd tried there that morning, but he wanted to go back and recheck it.

He came by the house about two hours later. Said nobody had seen Seth, of course. I was getting tired of hearing that phrase.

Then he said something else. He told me he'd stopped by the house after leaving the river, that he'd checked to see if all the guns were there, and that there wasn't one missing. Then I thought about what Son must have been feeling as he checked through the house and counted each gun, and I felt so for him, down to my unrested soul. But all the guns had been there. Thank the good Lord above.

After I gathered myself, which took a minute, I started to get up to go ahead and call the sheriff again, and that's when the phone rang. Son was the first one to it.

Michael

It was still desperate times for me, past desperate. Those bastards had rolled me and left me with hardly a dime. My electricity got cut off, the phone too, and then I got an eviction notice. It looked like I might lose the car. What I needed was a loan until I could get back on my feet. And I'd started thinking about maybe sending Frances a little money each month, that she could probably use it and that, well maybe I *had* to do something for her—for my own reasons.

The question was how to get money. No bank was going to give me a loan, that was for damn sure. I tried Granddaddy. Called him collect. He wanted to know where I was, like he was going to come get me or have me picked up or something.

"I'm in Panama City," I said, which at that very moment was the truth. "You could wire the money here."

I heard him take a long breath. "What kind of work are you doing?"

"Masonry," I told him.

"So you're learning a trade?"

"Yes, sir. You could say that."

"Well, is it the truth, or just something I could *say?*"

"It's the truth."

"How much do you need?"

215

"A thousand, maybe."

"That's a lot of money, Michael. Tell me why you need it."

"The truck has to have some work. It's not running."

"I don't think you're telling me the truth," he said, "and I'm certainly not going to send you any money. Why don't you come home? Either come up here, or go to Montgomery. Your mother's concerned about you."

"I can't leave my job. How about just five hundred?"

"No, Michael. Something tells me you've made some poor decisions," he said. "Now you've got to live with them. And what about the girl, and her child? Your child? What do you plan to do for them?"

"I don't know. Something."

"Have you forgotten about them?"

"No."

"So what are you going to do?"

"About what?"

"Your responsibilities."

"Bye," I said then and hung up. He wasn't going to help me. And I needed a whole lot more than a lecture.

Then I hit on a dangerous idea, but one I knew I could pull off. I'd just take a few little advances on my pay. Nothing anybody would have to know about. A little creative accounting, you might say. A little short count on the product, a little extra money for me. So that's what I did. Simple, so long as I didn't get greedy, which I didn't. And I knew there was always side work. Pretty soon the world would be right again, the moon full, the stars bright, the tides high, and the waves talking like a sweet woman drunk on rum.

Of course it didn't work out that way, though. Things have a way of getting found out, but when it's way past the dry and dusty time, and you're desperate enough, you convince yourself that they won't, that you can hide and cover up, but sometimes lies don't work, not when you're lying to someone who's better at it than you.

So my plans had to undergo a sudden change. It didn't matter anymore about the electricity or the phone or even the eviction notice. All that mattered was me taking my leave of the Sunshine State and my former business associates.

I headed north, taking the backroads that I knew like the palm of my hairy hand, then hit Montgomery and stayed with friends and former lady friends, but finally found myself moving on. I guess I thought I could go back to loading trucks. The money would get me by for a while, and by the time the lawyer, or anybody else, heard that I was in town, I'd be able to move on again with a little cash in my pocket and pay off my "loan." It wasn't *that* much.

Seth

I woke up early that Monday morning knowing what I had to do. It just came to me when my eyes opened, unless maybe it had already been in my dreams during the night. I didn't make any plans when the idea came. I just did it and didn't think. Sometimes you can't let yourself think.

I got up and got dressed and made sure all the money Granddaddy had paid me on Saturday was still in my billfold. Then right after Daddy left for work, I left too, about a half an hour earlier than usual. Erin's door was shut. And Kate was back in the kitchen banging dishes in the sink. She was the last person I wanted to see, not that she would have cared one way or another about what I was doing.

Instead of walking up the road toward the store, I turned and cut through the graveyard past the newer graves in front and headed for the woods and made my way through the clear places in the brush. Then I saw the old family plot and walked among the gray stones for a minute and tried to imagine what my great-great-grandfather and great-grandfather might think of me—and whether or not I could ever be the kind of man each of them must have been. I wondered what they might think about what I was doing and decided probably not very much, but I couldn't let dead people stop me.

At the corner of the graveyard, I cut out across an open field and away from our pasture and passed the little white house where Daddy had gone to school as a boy and where Grandmama had taught when she first moved to Riverfield, before she met Granddaddy. I made it to the highway in a few more minutes and hurried to be sure that I got off the road before Granddaddy came past.

I only had to stay on the pavement for a few hundred yards. A store owned by black people stood just off to the right on the other side of a ditch filled with water and broken bottles. I'd never been in it before. Hardly any white people ever went there. It was always closing down, then reopening. I knew it was open now and that buses stopped there to pick people up. I'd seen the names of the cities where they were headed on the front of them—Dallas, Memphis, New Orleans. Most white people went to Demarville to catch the bus, but I figured I could get on it here just as well.

The door was propped open and a fan blew from off to the side. A thin black woman stood behind the counter and watched me walk in. She didn't smile or say anything, just stared, like maybe she was in a bad mood. I didn't recognize her, so I figured that she didn't trade at our store and might not know who I was. I looked around real quick and didn't see anybody else. The place smelled like sweeping compound and kerosene, or coal oil as black people and some old people call it. There was a strong smell of ammonia, too. I didn't really feel like I belonged there, but I walked on up to the edge of the counter.

"Is there a bus going to Montgomery?" I said.

"Yeah," she said, and that was all.

"What time does it come?"

"Not till the afternoon."

"Are there any buses before that?"

"They one going to Tuscaloosa. Be here in about a half hour. You want that one?"

219

"How much is it?"

"Depends," she said, then started dusting the counter.

"On what?"

"One-way or two-way ticket?"

"One-way."

"Be eight dollars," she said.

She got the ticket ready and put it in a small envelope with Trailways written on the side of it. Then she took my money and gave me my change. I walked over and sat in a chair by the door. She kept dusting and would look at me every once in a while. She probably wondered why I didn't have a suitcase and why Tuscaloosa was as good as Montgomery. Or maybe she didn't wonder about anything at all. It didn't really matter. All that did matter was my getting on a bus before Granddaddy started looking for me.

It didn't take long. The bus got there a little early and pulled away at eight-twenty, after the bus driver drank a cup of coffee and checked his watch a few times.

We stopped in Valhia, then headed to Tuscaloosa. I knew it would be about an hour's ride and settled back in my seat and watched the woods and the fields pass by my window. I thought a lot about what Kate had done and tried to understand how she could think I would steal anything from her. It didn't make sense. And she'd looked at me so mean when she came in my room, like she hated me. She came back and made that apology, but Daddy had probably made her. He told me she'd been under a lot of strain, and even though that didn't excuse what she'd done, I should try to forgive her. I told him I would, but it wasn't that easy. I just didn't want to be around her, to have to see her look at me again the way she did that morning. Maybe that's one reason I got on the bus. She pushed me enough to make me go ahead and do it, and maybe that was a good thing, something I needed.

By the time we rolled up to the station in Tuscaloosa, it was almost ten-thirty and I hadn't eaten any breakfast yet. The way the black woman back at the store had looked at me, I hadn't wanted to have to buy anything else from her—like a sweet roll and a pint of milk maybe. So when I got off the bus and went inside, I found a vending machine and bought a couple of honey buns and drank a Coke with them.

After that I went up to the ticket window and asked about a bus to Montgomery. A gray-headed man smoking a cigar said one had left about forty-five minutes ago and that there wouldn't be another one until late that afternoon. I was just glad there *was* another one. For a minute I'd been afraid I would have to stay overnight and didn't know what in the world I would have done then. I went ahead and bought a ticket. It cost eleven dollars and that left me with about thirty.

On my way out of the station, I saw an older woman talking on a pay phone and thought about calling Grandmama and letting her know where I was and where I was going and that I was all right. I knew she'd be upset, more than upset, that they all would be, and part of me couldn't believe what I was doing, that I would make them worry, but if I'd called, Daddy might have checked the bus schedule and come up to Tuscaloosa to get me before the next bus, and I couldn't let anybody stop me, especially Daddy, for some reason. I had to forget about everybody else. They were just going to have to hurt for a while.

I did think about trying to call Mama, but I knew she would probably be at work. And for some reason I didn't want to talk to her before I saw her. It had been two whole years since I'd heard her voice. Maybe I was afraid she would sound like a stranger, or that I would.

There wasn't much to see or do downtown. I walked past office buildings and shoe stores and dime stores and men in suits and women carrying shopping bags and wearing high heels. It started to get pretty hot out, but a breeze blew every once in a while, and there was something about being by myself, nobody in the world knowing where I was, that made me feel free, like I could take a bus not just to Montgomery, but anywhere, and do anything I wanted. I'd never felt that way before in my life. Of course there were only thirty dollars in my pocket, but that didn't matter. It was the feeling that was important, and I wondered then if that was how Michael felt sometime, or all the time, and I thought maybe I understood him a little better.

Before long I was out of downtown and close to the university. The traffic got heavy and small crowds of students started walking past. They were laughing and talking. Classes must have let out. Most of the guys had long hair and the girls all wore shorts. They were pretty, with tan legs and their hair pulled up off their shoulders. I wished for a minute that Bobby had been with me so that he could see the campus and all the pretty girls going by and the big oaks that lined the sidewalks. I knew that one day I'd go to college, but Bobby probably wouldn't. He'd have to go to work.

I just kept walking. When I got tired, and hot, I went in a big building that turned out to be the library and found a cushioned chair and sat down and cooled off in the air-conditioning. I might have even gone to sleep for a little while, which really isn't like me.

There was a diner right off campus that I'd passed on my way in, and I walked back to it and ate a late lunch. Then I headed back downtown and found the bus station again and killed the last hour watching people come and go through the double doors.

Finally my bus was called over the PA system, and I went in the bathroom and rinsed my face and combed my hair, then walked out and found a seat on the bus. In about ten more minutes the driver got on and we pulled out of the terminal, headed toward Montgomery. And that's when I started to feel nervous, or maybe scared, in a way I hadn't before. It didn't have anything to do with Daddy or Grandmama and Granddaddy, either. It had to do with Mama.

I hadn't seen her in so long and suddenly I was afraid that she wouldn't want me showing up at her door, that she had a different life now, and that she'd had to put me out of her thoughts the way I'd tried to keep her out of mine. And maybe she was mad at me. After all, I was the one who'd told her I wouldn't be coming to Montgomery ever again. I remembered Daddy saying, "Do you want to see her?" And my telling him, "No." Then I'd written the letter, and everything had been so confusing, and now I still couldn't make sense out of what I'd been told or what I'd done, or been made to do.

Woods and power lines flashed past my bus window in the bright light of the late afternoon sun, and my thoughts and my memories seemed as tangled to me as the kudzu vines that smothered and choked the trees and bushes along the highway. Then I heard Frances' voice in my mind. "Don't worry. You'll see your mother again," she'd said and made it sound so simple, like all I had to do was exactly what I was doing. It could be that easy.

But she'd also said something else in Demarville that day that still confused me, or so I wanted to think. "Try not to be too mad at your father," she'd said. Maybe, though, I hadn't wanted to understand her then and didn't want to now as the bus rolled south because maybe I really did know what she meant and had known for a long time. The things I'd heard about Mama from Grandmama and Daddy had all been so terrible. Why had they told me such awful things? Why had I needed to know? Maybe it was because they hadn't wanted me to see her. Maybe Daddy's question about whether or not I wanted to see Mama hadn't been a question at all.

Suddenly I didn't feel so bad about disappearing, leaving them to worry and wonder about what had happened to me. After all, Granddaddy had told me once that he would give me the money to run away from Mama if I'd had to go live with her. He'd told me to take a bus, just like I was doing now. Maybe they should all have to suffer the way Mama would have had to if I'd run away from her, I thought, and then realized that maybe they were suffering the way Mama *did* have to suffer.

And what if she didn't want to see me? What if it all came to that?

The bus passed down out of the hills and woods we'd been in, and the highway grew straight and ran through open fields and cow pastures and past farm houses with wide front porches. Before long we pulled up to a gas station with two red new-looking pumps in front and a pile of used tires to one side. The driver announced "Maplesville" as he set the brakes and got out of his seat. There hadn't been any sign on the road that said Maplesville, and there didn't seem to be a town anywhere either. But two old women got off the bus and in a few minutes a boy about my age got on and sat in the seat across the aisle from me. He had short red hair and kept looking around like he was scared.

After we were about ten miles or so down the road, he turned toward me and said something that I didn't hear at first.

"What?" I said.

"Where you headed to? I'm going to Dothan, to see my grandparents."

"Atlanta," I heard myself say. "I've got a brother there."

He didn't say anything else after that. There was only the drone of the engine and the sound of the tires against the pavement.

I don't know why I lied. Maybe the truth of what I was doing was more than I could say to anyone.

Laura

That afternoon, while I sat out on the back porch after work and the sun turned the clouds to pale red, I made a decision that I'd been considering off and on for quite some time. I decided to sell the house and knew then that I should have done it much sooner. Sometimes you hold onto the familiar, no matter how painful.

Later I felt up to going to the grocery store, which took a while because I'd let myself run out of so many of the items I needed. Food and household necessities had been the last things on my mind. When I pulled back into the driveway it was near dark, almost dark enough for me not to have seen the figure of someone sitting on my front step. My first thought was that some neighborhood teenager was being very bold to sit in front of my house that way, and I hoped he wasn't going to be rude about leaving, but then he stood up and there was something about him that looked familiar. He took one step forward and I felt a jolt so strong that it was as if I were being awakened from some long sleep or unendurable dream.

I opened up the car door. "Mama?" he called, the sound of a question in his voice, and I wished there had been some way for me to answer so that there would never again be even the hint of a question when he said that word, no doubt ever as to who I was in his eyes. All I said was, "Yes," just that, but with an urgency that must have sounded strange to him. Or perhaps he understood after all.

I walked toward him, hardly aware of my steps or of the heavy purse hanging off my shoulder, and hugged him tightly to me there in the yard, not caring if any neighbors might be witness to one last little drama in front of the house—a drama in such quiet contrast to the sound of ambulance sirens like those from what was now years before.

He was so much bigger than the last time I'd seen him, taller and more broad. He felt a little like a stranger in my arms, and that made the tears come that I'd been holding back, tears for what had been lost. I did not try to stop them or hide them once they started.

"Are you all right?" I said, suddenly afraid that something terrible must have happened to make him come to me this way.

"I'm fine," he said. "I didn't know if it was you at first. You've got a new car."

"It's me," I said and looked at him in the last little bit of light. His eyes were wet and he tried to look away so that I wouldn't see. "It's all right," I said. "Tears don't matter. They're not unmanly."

I'd imagined many times the first moment when I might see him again, had pictured it happening in Valhia or maybe the bus station here. Sometimes I'd imagined him being close to the age he was now, or sometimes fully grown and maybe near finishing college or about to get married. I would have gotten a letter from him, or perhaps a phone call from a voice I wouldn't recognize, and we would have begun to get to know one another again through writing and talking, then made plans to meet. But now here he was, not at all as I'd imagined it, but I was just as happy, or maybe more so because of the suddenness of it.

I held him for a while longer, not wanting to speak again, not yet. Then he began to gently pull away from me, but still I wouldn't let go.

"Do you think we should go on inside," I said at last and hugged him tightly one more time.

We walked to the front door then and I got my keys out of my purse, and that was when I saw the light inside my car was on and saw that the door was still open and remembered the bags in the back seat. I smiled at the thought that even at such a time as this, the mundane has a way of creeping in. The daily chores still have to be done despite everything, and maybe that's as it should be, maybe that's what saves us.

"Come on and help me carry in the groceries," I said. "It'll only take a minute. Then I want to hear about how you got here."

We each took a bag and carried them inside, then went back for the rest, and doing that simple task with him felt familiar, as if it were an evening from three or four years before and I was taking him away from watching television to help me unload groceries, just the way we did every week, only now he didn't complain and could carry the heavy bags so much more easily.

After putting things away in the kitchen, at least the things that had to be refrigerated, we sat down in the den. Seth took the sofa. I sat in my chair. He kept looking around, perhaps to see if I'd changed the house any, and he probably noticed small differences—a new print here, a new table there—that marked for him the passage of time and the changes that had taken place in our lives.

"How did you get here?" I said. "And why don't you have a suitcase with you?"

"I caught the bus at a store in Riverfield. It was kind of a sudden thing. I didn't take the time to pack. Then I took a cab from the station downtown."

"What are you telling me here? Does your father know where you are?"

He looked down at the floor. "No. None of them know." He paused a moment and slowly looked up again, his eyes now filled with a kind of light I had not seen in them before. "I just left," he said, and a trace of anger that I couldn't help but be proud of registered in his voice.

I went and sat down beside him then and took his hand, wrapping his fingers in mine, feeling their moisture and warmth, and then felt unsure as to what to say next, whether to praise or to condemn. I'd suspected what he'd done when I first saw he didn't have any kind of bag with him, and now hearing him confirm my suspicions made me realize with such a sense of wholeness that he'd never stopped needing me, that I was still his mother and even though we'd lost time, we hadn't lost everything, that some ties can't be severed, no matter the words or the actions of others, and no matter their reasons for either.

"I'm glad you came," I said finally, "however you had to do it. But you have to call and let your father know where you are. Don't be like your brother and just run."

"Could you call him for me?" he said, fidgeting slightly, like a child would.

"I told you a little while ago that tears aren't unmanly, but not doing what you know you should do is. You've got to be responsible. There are things that other people just can't do for you. And you shouldn't ask them." I realized, of course, that I sounded like my father.

"But I don't know if I want to talk to him right now, or any of them," he said, his voice rising a little.

"Why? Can you tell me?"

And here is where the terrible details of my history came out, all the things I'd hoped he would never learn but knew with little doubt that he *had* learned. I'd wanted to have some time with him before having to deal with the past, but perhaps he simply couldn't wait to speak what was on his mind. He'd already had to wait far too long.

"They said things. Did things," he said, an urgency in his voice now.

"What things?" I readied myself.

"They told me . . ." He turned away then and stared at the picture of the room reflected by the darkened window. He would have to have help, I saw.

"Things about me?"

He nodded his head.

"That I tried to hurt myself?"

He nodded again.

"That I took sleeping pills?"

"Yes," he said in a forced whisper.

I took a breath. "It's true. And I'm sorry. But that's been a long while ago now. Years. I was sick, but I'm well now." And then I added, hesitantly, just as quietly as he had spoken, "I hope you can forgive me."

He still would not turn toward me. He only nodded his head again and squeezed my hand, but the language of his touch said enough, said more than I could ever thank him for.

"What else did they tell you?" I asked then, pushing, knowing that he needed to say it all. "That I wasn't a good mother?"

"Yes," he said, just as softly as before, as if there were someone in the room who he was afraid might overhear.

"Well, there was a time when I couldn't be. Sometimes we just can't do the things we want to. We have to wait. But when I started to fight for you, I was ready again to be the kind of mother you deserved. My love for you never changed, though. That was the one constant. Can you understand what I'm saying?"

He finally turned toward me. His brown eyes were wet again, but he didn't look away this time. His skin had the slightest flush of red in it from being upset, and his mouth was drawn into such a tight line. "Yes," he said slowly. "I think so."

I let go of his hand then. "Even though your father and grandparents did things you wished they hadn't, you still have to make your call," I said. "All of us have to get past the things our parents do. You're no different. And the things they do in the name of love are usually the hardest to get beyond. Believe me, I know."

"Can I stay awhile before I go back?" he said.

"Of course. I hoped you would. We'll get you some more clothes to wear tomorrow."

He went into the kitchen and called. I didn't try to overhear and he spoke so quietly that it would have been impossible. I hoped that his father wouldn't be too angry with him, then decided, knowing him as I did, that he would only feel relief at the sound of his son's voice.

He came back into the room after a few minutes. "I talked to Kate first," he said. "She told me he was at Grandmama and Granddaddy's house. So I called down there and he answered."

"What did he say?"

"That he was glad I was all right, and that he never would have thought I'd do something like this. He sounded disappointed in me."

"Does that bother you?" I said.

"Not as much as you might think. I'm still glad I did what I did," he said, his voice rising a little again.

The next day I took off from work and took him shopping. Then late that afternoon he went and saw a few old friends in the neighborhood, but when he came home he seemed down. They had probably changed more than he'd expected, were no longer children, as when he'd last seen them, just as he was no longer a child.

I told him the following afternoon that I was probably going to sell the house, and it seemed okay with him. "It's just not the same around here anymore, is it?" he said.

He stayed until the end of the week. I was hoping he would stay through the weekend since I'd only been able to take off the one day, but I think a part of him couldn't put off any longer going back and facing his father and his grandparents. I respected this but was of course disappointed, wanting more time to get to know him again, or rather, to get to know the person he'd become, but I knew that it would take more than just a few more days for this. Instinct told me it was best not to push, and there was no doubt in my mind that we would have more time together. Seth had forced a change that could not be altered or amended, not by anyone.

At lunch on Friday I took him back to the bus station, a place I'd last seen two years before when we'd had to part, a time when so much was at stake and so much was unknown, and now when his bus pulled away, with the sun so bright against the windows, I was not overcome by fears but was filled with something that might be called expectancy.

This feeling stayed with me for days afterward, and was not even broken, at least not completely, by the sound of Michael's disturbed voice on the phone late one night. If I had been able to make more sense out of what he said, though, if I had known what would soon happen to him, then his call would have been more upsetting, and *maybe* I could have done something for him. As it was, I had mostly grown immune to his poor drunken riddles. If only he had spoken the truth, for once.

Conrad

His bus was early and he was standing out in front of the station with a small canvas bag at his feet when I pulled up. He didn't see me at first and he leaned against the side of the building and stuck his hands in his pockets, then squinted his eyes against the sun and the heat, which were both so intense you could see those waves of vapor coming off the asphalt in the distance, the way they do when the temperature reaches so high that the tar melts.

Then he turned and saw me, his eyes still just as squinted, even though he had turned away from the sun, and it struck me that I'd seen him look this way once before, when I'd had to go pick him up on the Square in Valhia, right before Michael had disappeared. And just like then, his expression, his stance, seemed angry and at such odds with the boy he had always been.

I got out of the car with some hesitation. "How are you?" I said and took his bag for him. It was as simple a gesture as I could make at a moment that seemed to call for simple gestures.

"All right," he said and got in the car while I put his bag inside the trunk.

I then got behind the wheel, unsure of what to say next, as lost really for words as I had ever been and so afraid that one wrong word might do untold damage to the most precious of things in my life.

"How is your mother?" I finally said, and it seemed so clumsy, as if I had no right to ask.

"She's fine," he said. "She's going to sell the house." His tone was mostly flat, but there was a trace of something in it that sounded like fear, and the realization that he was afraid of me in some way was a wound to the heart as deep as any weapon could inflict.

"It's all right, Seth," I said. "I'm not going to punish you, if that's what you're thinking. I only wish you'd let me know what you wanted. Or had maybe left me a note at least."

He didn't respond. I put the car in gear and pulled into the traffic and then turned right at the next light.

"I missed her," he said suddenly after a few blocks.

"Yes," I said, not knowing what else to say, too afraid that anything more would have sounded false. I just drove.

About halfway home, as we passed between cotton fields burning in the sun and hay pastures being cut, I brought up what I knew would be a difficult subject. "I'm sorry about what happened with Kate," I said, "that business about the watch, I mean."

"I didn't steal it," he said.

"I know. She's sorry about it. I don't understand why she would do something like that, but I've talked to her about it some more. She knows beyond any doubt now that you wouldn't steal anything. She should have already realized it, but it won't happen anymore. Her watch probably got lost in the move somehow," I said, though I really felt that Erin had probably taken it and that Kate simply couldn't bring herself to accept the fact. But I didn't say any of this to Seth.

"It must have been upsetting to you," I said after a moment of silence. "Being accused that way."

"It was. I didn't do it."

"I know. I'm sorry it happened. Things seemed to be getting so much better around the house. They will again. I promise. It's an adjustment. Just give it some time."

He remained quiet, looking out the window, his hands gripping his knees as if he might collapse if he let go.

"Is what happened with Kate the reason you left?"

"Partly," he said, and that was all. Neither of us were ready to take it any further, and we simply rode home quietly, made mute by our fears.

Kate wasn't at home when we arrived, which must have been a relief to Seth. Erin wasn't home either.

Seth went first to his room, carrying his new bag. Then he came back up to the front of the house and walked out onto the porch. The fact that it was so hot outside told me how much he wanted to be alone, or at least away from me, figuring probably that I wouldn't want to be out in the heat. So I didn't bother him.

He stayed for a while in the swing on the porch, which is where I used to go as a boy sometimes to be alone and think, and when he eventually came back inside, I asked if he'd like to go down to see his grandparents later.

"Not tonight," he said.

I started to tell him how worried they'd been, how much they'd missed him, but didn't. Then he said something that sounded like himself.

"I guess I should work in the store in the morning, though. It'll be Saturday and Granddaddy will be busy."

But I knew that if he didn't see his grandfather tonight, he wouldn't want to have to face him in front of customers in the morning.

"Actually, I've got an errand to run tomorrow that you could help me with," I said. "If you wouldn't mind. I could let your grandfather know that I needed you."

He nodded his head. "That would be all right. What kind of errand?"

"I need to go over near Gainesville. There's an old man there who can repair some of these shutters on the house that are in such bad shape. I can borrow your grandfather's truck and you could help me load them. And the old man says he's got some hardware for these doors, hinges and doorknobs, that might match what we've got. Some of these need replacing."

The expression on his face made it clear that he didn't really want to make that long a trip with me; but the alternative, having to face his grandparents that night, or his grandfather the next morning, maybe his grandmother too if she worked, must have seemed more daunting. After all, he'd already faced me, that part was over with, and he must have wanted to put off facing the two of them as long as he could.

"All right," he said. "I can go with you."

"Good, but you know you'll have to see you grandparents sometime in the next few days."

"I know."

He started to go back out onto the front porch it appeared, but we both heard the sound of a car door slam and, in a minute, Kate came walking into the living room carrying a bag or two from the dollar store in Demarville.

"I needed a few things," she said. "I got my hair done too." She looked at Seth then as if she were embarrassed. "Did you have a good visit with your mother?"

"Yes," he said.

"Well, good. Seth, I'm sorry about what happened between us before you left. Sometimes I let things get to me. I hope you can forgive me."

"It's all right," he said.

"Thank you," she said and walked toward the hall. I knew that the tension between them hadn't suddenly vanished, but I hoped they'd made a start, at least.

Late that night, lying in bed listening to the bark of a neighbor's dog, one maybe out hunting for himself in the woods nearby, I remembered Seth telling me that Laura planned to sell the house, and I couldn't help recalling our history there. I'd had such hopes for us, and even though it was no longer my house, and hadn't been for two years, I still felt, oddly enough, as if something had come to an end. But how can something end twice?

And here I was in another house, the house where I was born, about to repair shutters and door knobs and hinges, which was really the least of what needed to be done, and now there were all these other kinds of repairs to think about. But perhaps some repairs are never complete. Human relationships are far more complex than carpentry or masonry, and we are all such un-skilled laborers. Maybe time, the very thing that does such dam-age to a house, is the only thing that can repair the people who live within it. Yet we can't just sit waiting. We have to try our hand.

The next morning I went up to the store and got my father's truck, without Seth, then came back and the two of us loaded the shutters, working mostly in silence, so it didn't take long. By nine o'clock we were headed toward Gainesville along rough county roads that were mostly deserted. Neither of us said very much still, and Seth finally reached over and turned the radio on, though he at least kept the volume turned down fairly low.

After about ten miles we lost the station and he couldn't find another, not one he liked, anyway. So then there was only quiet again in the truck, which I broke.

"How do you feel about painting?" I said.

"Painting what?"

"The outside of the house, after the summer, when it cools off a little."

"You want me to help?"

"Yes. I'd appreciate it."

"I've never painted anything before."

"That's all right. It's not hard, just hard work. But it needs it. The wood needs protecting."

"All right," he said. He didn't ask what colors we'd use or how long it would take or how many gallons of paint we'd need. I let it drop.

We found the house just this side of Gainesville, before we crossed the river into Sumter County. We unloaded the shutters beneath a shed that the old man showed us. He walked with a limp, and we slowly followed him to another outbuilding full of junk, where I found door knobs and hinges that matched the ones at the house, or at least as closely as I could expect to find.

"I see you got your boy with you," he said as I sorted through junk. "That's mighty fine. I bet he's a big help."

"Yes, sir," I said. "He is."

"Don't seem like the young people care much about helping their parents these days. Not from what I can see."

"No, sir," I said. "Sure doesn't."

"I raised my grandboy up. Me and my wife. Raised him right. He turned out to be about as sorry as they come."

"I hate to hear that," I said.

The old man just looked away and shrugged his shoulders, as if it was something he'd accepted, like a bad summer drought. Seth and I began to gather the hardware I wanted.

Instead of heading back home, I drove across the river bridge and right into Gainesville. We stopped at a little country store and drank a Coke and I put some gas in the truck. Seth didn't say very much or offer to pump the gas. Then we headed back toward the river, but instead of crossing it, I surprised him by pulling off the road at a little park just before the bridge. I came to a stop under a cedar tree right next to an old gazebo. He asked what we were doing, and I told him there was something that I wanted to show him. He didn't ask any more questions.

We got out and he reluctantly followed me across the road and up a hill to a small monument surrounded by an iron fence.

237

"So where are we?" he said.

"This is the site where Nathan Bedford Forrest and his men finally laid down arms," I said, "what was left of them after the battle for Selma, and all the other battles they'd been in, like Shiloh and Chickamauga. Lee had already surrendered a month before at Appomattox."

I checked the date to see if I'd remembered it correctly. I had—May 9th. Seth read it too, standing quietly beside me, and as I glanced at him for a moment, at his downcast eyes and intent expression, I wondered why I had suddenly wanted to come here. I hadn't thought about it before we left that morning, and I hadn't even seen it in years, but as we'd driven over, something in my mood had called up from my memory this place of final defeat.

"They considered Mexico," I said. "Forrest and some of his men. They couldn't stand the idea of having to surrender, but Forrest decided not to leave the country, and his men followed suit. He decided to act with grace, you might say. And in his farewell address, he told them it was their duty to give up animosities and private differences, no matter how difficult."

"Must have been pretty hard for them," Seth said and took a step away from the monument.

"Yes. Especially for a man like Forrest, who was so fierce. He was wounded four times and had twenty-nine horses shot out from beneath him. Once, when he had Federal forces in front of and behind him, an aide asked him what they were going to do. 'Divide in half and fight in both directions,' he said. And in any picture of him, you can't help being struck by his power and by the notion that here was a man who achieved whatever he willed, no matter how hard he had to be on others and no matter how much grief he caused. Your great-great-grandfather rode with him for a period of time, you know. And he had quite a few horses shot out from beneath him, too."

"Yes, I know," Seth said, sounding a little bored.

"Of course, Forrest was too hard on others," I said then, beginning to realize by this point that I probably sounded as if I were giving some sort of lecture. "He wasn't the kind of man you want to be around. But in time of war, maybe you need a man like him. Not that he was always harsh."

The cloud cover had been heavy most of the morning, with the sun only breaking through every once in a while, but now it broke through again, partially, and cast the field in a light that wasn't too hard but still so brightly illuminated Seth's features, his too-long hair that was growing darker, his brown eyes that were again downcast, his lips, slightly parted and shaped as if he were about to speak but didn't know how to begin. When he finally looked up at me, and even held my gaze for a moment, I wondered what he saw in my own sun-lit features, if my expression told him anything beyond the words I'd just said, or if he saw reflected only his own inability to speak of what lay between us. But of course it wasn't his responsibility to speak. It was mine.

For a moment I thought about all those soldiers, about the despair they must have felt for their failure, or their perceived failure, and all that they had lost as they struck their tents for the last time. But of course it was my own failures and losses that really concerned me while I stood there beginning to sweat beneath the sun's heat. I'd lost a wife whom I loved still, an adopted son I'd hoped to raise properly, and a daughter I'd never claimed as my own the way I should have. And like those soldiers from so long ago, who at least had families to go home to, there was nothing left for me to do but accept what could no longer be denied.

Here I was, in this modern world with so many families in pieces, trying to make another family, and was about to lose my son. In fact, he began walking away from me and toward the truck, as if he knew my fear and wanted to confirm it, and this time I followed him, trying to catch up the way a child might.

I walked across the field, coming closer and closer to him, to his turned back, all the while searching for the right words to say, and they came to me finally from the place where I should have expected them to come.

The shade of the cedar barely covered the truck, and I caught up with him and opened my door just as he opened his. We both climbed in and before I even thought of starting the engine, I put my hands on the steering wheel, gripped it tightly, as if it were some form of support, and looked out across the road from where we had just come, then shut my eyes and uttered the same words that Lee had spoken to his men at Gettysburg as they returned from the horrible and bloody failure that was Pickett's charge. "The blame is mine," I said.

May

Seth and his daddy came over Sunday night. Kate didn't come with them. She had to take Erin to town so that Erin could go see a movie with her cousins. As soon as Seth came in the door I could see how nervous he felt from the look in his eyes. He was probably afraid that we were going to be upset with him still, which his granddaddy and I were at first. But Conrad had said to me more than once early that morning, in a tone he doesn't usually take, that it was his daddy's place to talk to him about what he'd done.

It took some courage for Seth to do what he did, to go off that way, and so at supper I decided maybe I'd better have some courage too, if that's the right word.

"Seth," I said after we'd sat down at the table and passed everything around, "we're glad you saw your mother and we hope you had a good visit with her."

There was a long quiet, like right after a preacher's final prayer, then Seth took another piece of cornbread, probably just out of nervousness seeing as how he already had two pieces on his plate. "Yes, ma'am," he said finally. "We had a good visit." Then he looked over at me and added, "I've missed her," which I knew must have been hard for him to say, but I could understand why he said it. He didn't turn away from me, but held my eyes with a look that lasted only a moment, but was a little longer than I would have expected from him; and I felt afraid then for what he might know but wouldn't understand.

"Reckon you want to earn a little more money before school starts back?" his granddaddy said then. It was just the kind of thing that needed to be said and at just the right time. Sometimes Conrad surprises me.

"Yes, sir," Seth said.

"Well, I could sure use the help. You'll be there in the morning then?"

"Yes, sir. I promise."

"Good," he said.

"Yesterday we went over to the site where Forrest surrendered," Son said. "I hadn't been there in years."

"Did y'all have a good time?" I said.

He looked over at Seth and Seth nodded his head a little, and I wondered how things had really gone for them on their trip, but I knew only time would tell.

In bed that night I said several prayers after turning out my lamp. I said one for Seth and his daddy, and one for Seth and his mother. And then I asked Him to help guide us and do what was right for our children and to please forgive us when we did wrong.

Michael

My little one-man parade hit Valhia the middle of August, after I left Montgomery. I went through Selma on the way, but did not stop to see my father and didn't even think about why. Once I got to Valhia, I crashed at a friend's place, a guy called Goose from down at the loading dock at Browning and Ford's. I figured he was called that because he had a long neck, but I never asked him. Old Goose could be just a little bit mean, but he never was to me.

He lived in a camphouse with a tin roof and tarpaper sides that sat down beside the Black Fork and had been flooded no telling how many times. You could see the water stains on the walls inside. But it was good and dry the night I got there, and we had a high old time the first couple of days, eating fresh catfish off his trotline and watching barges and pushboats float past.

I figured I'd better live outside of town for however long I stayed, and that I'd best keep away from the Square. And Granddaddy, I knew, wouldn't recognize my car if he passed me on the road. All I had to do was go back to work loading trucks, keep myself out of sight, and save up a little money to pay back my "loan." But maybe going back to loading trucks wasn't the smartest thing I ever did. I don't know for sure, but the same guy who first put me onto my former business associates in Florida must have put them onto me, because they soon came calling.

I'd worked for about two weeks, had gotten in a little overtime even, and had cashed my first paycheck that afternoon. Goose and I decided to cook steaks on the grill that night, but when we got ready to put them on, we couldn't find any charcoal. He said he'd run back into town and that he'd pick up some more beer too. So I just sat outside, drank my beer, and watched the river, even talked to it a little bit.

After Goose left, I didn't hear any other car, so they must have already been close by, waiting to catch me alone. I didn't recognize the first one who came up the steps, but I did the second one. I'd worked with him in Florida. He was dark headed and always irritated. The other was blond with a crooked nose. Both of them were tall and built well, better than me. I told them I could give them two hundred now and pay the rest over the next three or four months, but they weren't in a mood to negotiate. They just shook their heads. I didn't say anything else. No way was I going to beg.

They got close up on me, and I swung and landed a good right on the jaw of the blond one just before they pinned me against the tarpaper wall. The blond guy smiled at me big enough to show his bad teeth. Then I was nothing but a punching bag spitting blood.

After I fell down to my knees, one of them, I don't know which, took my wallet and told me to have the rest in two weeks. Then they kicked me a few times, hard, and I thought for a minute about those two bastards down on the beach who'd rolled me that time. At least *they* hadn't beaten me too bad, but now I was getting tired of being beaten up. It hurts more than just your body.

Goose found me where I'd dropped and took me to the emergency room, not that I really remember it all that well, but what I do remember is waking up, my face and stomach and ribs hurting like the nurses must have taken a few extra shots at me to pass the time, and before I could even look down and see the bandages and the wrapping on me, there was Granddaddy's face right in mine, close enough for me to see the dark pupils of his eyes and to smell the mint on his breath. It about made me sick.

"So this is what it's come to?" he said.

"It appears that way, doesn't it?" I said. He never did like to have one of his questions answered with one of mine. He just looked away.

"Does this have anything to do with your needing money when you called last time?"

"Not a thing. Not a thing in the world."

"You're lying, Michael," he said, looking down into my face again. "You owe somebody money, probably for something illegal, maybe drugs, and they beat you up. Pretty badly, *it appears.*"

"No, that's not it. I got beaten up in a bar. That's all. Just a bar fight. A tough one," I said, starting to feel myself believe it. "I was talking with some guy's girlfriend, this blond girl, but I didn't know she was with anybody."

"So it wasn't really your fault?"

"Not really."

"What kind of fool do you take me for, Michael?"

"No kind."

"That's right. Now why don't you tell the police what happened? Tell them whatever it is you've been doing."

This time I was the one who looked away and didn't answer.

"That's right. Don't say anything. At least you won't be telling another lie."

I tried to move further away from him in the bed and just about cussed out loud it hurt so bad.

"Do you want to keep on with your life this way, running from family, getting beaten up, or do you want something else? Think about it. Try to show some intelligence for once."

He turned and walked out of the room and I heard his foot-steps down the hall for a minute, then didn't hear anything but the wheels of a cart roll by, probably a nurse wanting some-body's blood, and I hoped she wasn't coming for mine.

Sometime in the night I woke up hurting. Whatever they'd given me for pain after Granddaddy left must have worn off, washed right out of me along with my sweat. So I lay still, lis-tened to the sound of muffled voices in the hall, voices that made me feel like somebody was out there saying something they didn't want me to hear, and wondered how long I could last be-fore calling a nurse to give me something else for the pain in my sides and in my gut.

But pain pills isn't all I thought about. I wondered long and hard why I hadn't stopped in Selma to see my old man when I'd gone less than two blocks past his bar on the way from Mont-gomery. Hell, I knew as sure as I hurt inside that it would have been smarter to have *stayed* there, or anywhere else, than to come on to Valhia, where people knew me. But maybe I'd wanted Granddaddy to find me, to hear I was back. Maybe I was tired of being so cut off from everybody. Or it could have been that I wanted to be tracked down and get my beating over with. And why would I have stopped in Selma, anyway? I hadn't called and asked my father for any money because I knew he wouldn't give me any, just like I knew he wouldn't put me up in Selma, not even for a night. What can a son expect from a father? How much can he ask for? How much does he deserve? Damn if I know the answers. But I did know, down in my gut, that I would stop there again, when I could walk in with my head up and with money in my pocket, and I'd stay long enough for him to take off those goddamn sunglasses so I could have at least one good look at the man, right square into his eyes, and maybe see just how much of him there was in me.

But what right did I have to judge him? I was a father, too, and hadn't even seen my child, not once, much less done anything for it, or the mother. I'd have to do something for them before I'd face him again. I'd have to do something to make myself a man again.

Finally I buzzed the nurse and she came in and told me she couldn't give me anything yet, which was what I knew she'd say. So I kept lying there awake and every once in a while I'd try to shift a little in the bed, but it only made me hurt. There's something about a bad hurt that makes you feel like a child, like you can't do anything more for yourself than a child can. And then I wondered, just like a child, if my mother would come to see her boy, and I'm almost ashamed to say that I prayed she would.

Seth

I worked at the store until about ten o'clock that morning.
There weren't many customers, but the meat truck delivered
and I wrapped and weighed chickens until Daddy came by and
picked me up. Granddaddy already knew I was leaving early, but
we didn't talk about why. Just as Daddy pulled up in front of the
store, though, Granddaddy walked back to where I was working
and looked at me over the top of his glasses, which is what he always does when he's about to say something he wants you to be
sure to hear. "Don't worry about him too much. From the little
I've seen of him over the years, I bet he can take a beating pretty
well, probably give one, too. He's tough. I bet it wasn't a fair
fight."

"I'm not worried about him," I said, which was the truth, not
that I hadn't been thinking about Michael all morning. Granddaddy Tyner had called from Valhia early and told Daddy where
Michael was.

Daddy came inside then and said he wanted to check the oil in
the car before we left, and I told him I'd do it for him since my
hands were already sticky from wrapping chickens. He seemed a
little surprised that I'd volunteered, but I didn't mind doing it. I
went outside with a rag and ended up adding a quart. Then I
washed up and we were ready.

248

He drove slow out to the highway, having to watch for the bad
pot holes that gravel trucks had made, but somehow he managed to hit a few of them anyway. Then he waited longer than he
needed to before pulling out onto the highway, and I had to tell
him it was clear before he made the turn. He just didn't seem to
be paying attention.

We rode along without saying much, and finally I could see
how worried he was by the way he looked so hard at the road
and by how tight he held the steering wheel with both hands.
They looked so big and strong to me, and I remembered then
how we used to play that game when I was little where I'd try to
touch his palm and pull away before he could catch me in his
grip. I'd always wished that I was as strong and wondered now if
I was even close and if I would be quick enough to pull away in
time.

But grabbing hands had only been a game we'd played when I
was little, and what was really on my mind as we drove was
Michael, just like I knew he was on Daddy's mind, too.

Granddaddy had gotten it wrong, though. I wasn't worried
about Michael being hurt. What worried me was how Michael
might act toward Daddy, what he might say or do to hurt him.
I'd started thinking about it when I was getting dressed to go to
the store. And imagining Michael saying something hateful,
imagining him calling Daddy "Conrad" with that tone of voice
he'd used before, or refusing to shake his hand, or maybe even
cussing him, suddenly had made me mad enough to want to beat
him myself, to put bruises and welts on his face. And as I looked
at my father sitting next to me and saw again how worried he
was about seeing Michael, I got so mad at Michael for what he
might do that all the muscles in my arms and shoulders and chest
tightened and my hands almost shook. He didn't have any right
to talk ugly to my father or to put him down or make him feel
bad.

I looked out at the fields and pastures going by then, all just as green as they could be, and my eyes started to burn and my chest got so tight that I had to take a deep breath, and suddenly I hated more than anything in the world that I'd ever had to hurt my father the way I did, and I couldn't believe how he had forgiven me.

"Are you all right?" Daddy said then.

"I'm fine," I said.

"You know, I don't know what Michael will think when he sees us, or me, rather, but he might need us right now. And if he does then we ought to be there."

"Yes, sir," I said.

Before long we passed the city limit sign and then made the Square, and in a few more minutes we were parked at the hospital and my stomach drew up inside almost like I'd been hit.

After we went in the main door, Daddy asked a nurse behind a desk where Michael's room was and we walked down a hall that smelled like someone had just washed the floor and walls with ammonia and I had to take a deep hard breath again. Daddy knocked a few times, then pushed the door open.

Michael was awake, but it was hard to tell right away because his eyes were about swollen shut and he didn't move any or even say anything. His face looked worse than I'd imagined. It wasn't just his eyes that were swollen, so was his jaw, and there were bruises that didn't look like any colors I'd ever seen before but made me think about rotten plums that had broken open.

You'd think seeing him look that way would have made me feel sorry for him, but it didn't. Not all that much, anyway. At least not enough for me to forgive him if the first words out of his mouth were something ugly toward my father. But they weren't.

"Do I look all that bad?" he said, like a joke almost, like he'd been planning what to say because he'd known we were coming, which he couldn't have.

"I've seen you looking better," Daddy said. "Do you mind a little company?"

250

"No, I don't mind. I can't say I'd recommend staying the night, though. This is about the sorriest damn hotel I've ever stayed in."

"I bet it is," Daddy said, forcing a smile.

We both stood beside his bed by this time and I could see bruises on Michael's arms.

"What do you think, Seth?" he said.

"About what?"

"Did you ever think your brother would lose a fight this bad?"

"No. I don't guess so."

"Did they break any ribs?" Daddy said.

Michael nodded his head.

"So there was more than one?"

"Yes," he said. "More than one. If it had been only one, I might have lost, but I wouldn't look like this. You taught me better than that. Do you remember?"

"I remember. I didn't know if you would."

"Seth, has Conrad taught you how to use your fists when you have to?"

This time when he said Daddy's name it still sounded a little strange, but it didn't sound mean. I wished that he would call him Daddy, like he used to, but I guess he couldn't anymore.

"Yes," I said. "He taught me a long time ago."

"I figured he had. He taught me too. There were some boys who used to pick on me, older boys. This was probably a few years after you were born. Conrad took me out in the backyard and showed me how to stand and how to throw a punch. And how to protect myself. He even bought me a punching bag. I did all right after that."

"Yes, you did," Daddy said. "I watched you one time. From a distance."

Michael looked surprised. "Why don't y'all have a seat?" he said then.

Daddy and I walked around to the other side of the bed and

sat down in two green chairs that looked like they'd come out of some old barbershop. Things got kind of quiet for a while. Nobody had anything to say, I guess. I knew I didn't. Part of me was just so surprised that Michael wasn't acting ugly, and maybe that disappointed me some. Maybe I wanted my brother to act mean so that I could be mad at him, or stay mad at him. But being there in the room, seeing him again, it was almost like he hadn't ever done all those things he'd done. But how can you forget such bad things?

"What can we get for you?" Daddy said finally.

"Nothing that I can think of right now."

We were all quiet again and things were beginning to get uncomfortable. I could hear people walking up and down the hall and doctors being paged. Some man started coughing in a room across from us and it didn't sound like he'd ever stop.

Then Daddy asked Michael if he'd gone back to working on a tug, but Michael didn't seem to want to talk about what he'd been doing back down in Florida. The only thing he was clear about was that no, he hadn't been back on a tug, but that he missed it. Daddy kept asking him questions, and he'd look at Daddy, then at me, then back at Daddy. He'd only answer halfway, but not like he was trying to be mysterious or play some game, more like he was afraid to answer.

"Seth," Daddy said after a while, "would you mind if I talked to Michael for a few minutes? Just the two of us? Then we can all visit some more."

"No, I don't mind," I said, not sure if I really meant it.

He gave me some change to get a Coke and some crackers, and I walked out into the hall and closed the door behind me real slow. I wanted to stand there and listen to what they had to say to each other, but decided that maybe some things do need to be private after all.

The Coke and vending machines were down at the end of the hall and after I spent my change, I went out the side door and walked around to the lawn near the parking lot and leaned against an oak tree. I watched people come and go and ate my crackers. One woman came out with her little boy walking beside her. When they got to the edge of the parking lot, she took his hand and told him to be careful when he stepped off the curb, but he tripped anyway and she had to catch him with both hands. She looked so scared for a second. I wondered if maybe they'd been in to see the boy's father, and I imagined them a little family of three and hoped the father wasn't too sick.

After a while I went back in and walked up and down the halls for a little bit, not that the hospital in Valhia is really all that big. I kept passing the same nurses who looked at me like I shouldn't be wandering around the way I was, but none of them did anything more than give me strange looks. Off one hall a storage room door was open, and inside I saw more wheelchairs and crutches than I thought any hospital would ever need. All the wheelchairs were folded together and lined up against the walls and metal crutches hung on hooks. It all made me feel like there must be more injured people in the world than I'd ever thought about.

I kept walking around and couldn't help but wonder what Michael and Daddy were talking about. Maybe Frances, I thought, whether or not Michael was going to do anything to help her with her baby. Or maybe Daddy was trying to find out why he'd been beaten up so bad.

Finally I went back to the room and opened the door just a crack. There weren't any voices and I walked on in. Michael was lying in the same position as before, but Daddy wasn't in the room.

"Where'd Daddy go?" I said, feeling a little nervous all of a sudden.

"I don't know. I guess he'll be back in a few minutes. Come on and sit down. Tell me how you've been."

"He didn't say where he was going?"

"No. He didn't say. Maybe to look for you. Maybe to get a Coke. Who knows? He'll probably be right back, though."

Something about the tone of his voice and the way he looked at me told me Michael was lying, but I couldn't figure out why he would lie about such a little thing. It didn't make sense. I wondered for a minute if he'd made Daddy mad.

"Is Daddy all right?" I said.

He opened his eyes a little wider and cocked his head, like he was thinking about what I was really asking. "He's fine. We had a good talk. Don't you worry."

I believed him. Then I wondered if maybe he and Daddy were both trying to keep something from me. Maybe Daddy didn't want me to know where he'd gone and that's why Michael was lying. I sat down and hoped I'd find out soon enough.

"So, do you have a girlfriend yet?" Michael said.

"No."

"Well, there must be some girl you like."

"There was one, but she moved away," I said and looked away from him. I felt like I was telling him a secret, or at least part of one. I wasn't about to say who she was, but maybe he could guess.

"Did you tell her you liked her before she left?"

"No, but she probably knew."

"Now you listen to me. That's not good enough. If you like a girl, you've got to tell her. You hear me. You're getting too old to be bashful."

"You're right," I said. Then I told him something he probably didn't know. "I saw Mama not too long ago."

"How is she?" he said and his voice got real quiet.

"She's fine. She's going to sell the house."

"Really?" he said. He sounded surprised and a little sad. "I guess that makes sense, doesn't it?"

"Yes."

There was one other thing I had to mention, but I was afraid. Like he'd said though, I was getting too old to be bashful.

"What about Frances?" I said.

He studied me a minute. "I'm going to do what I can."

Before I could ask what that would be, Daddy came walking back in the room. He saw me and walked right to the bedside table where a pitcher of water sat and opened the drawer. There was some small piece of light blue paper folded up in his hand and he slipped it into the drawer.

"Thank you," Michael said.

Daddy just nodded his head and glanced at me for a second. I didn't ask any questions, but figured he'd been out to the car to get a check. I guess Michael needed money.

He sat down in the same chair again and clasped his hands over one knee and let out a breath, like he'd just finished something important, something he'd been wanting to do for a long time, maybe. "Did y'all have a little time to visit?" he said then.

"Yes," I said.

"It's good to see the both of you together. Too bad it's not under better circumstances."

"That's the truth," Michael said.

They talked some after that about who Michael's doctor was and about whether or not he'd get out the next morning. Then I saw the door begin to swing open and just like I'd known that morning after Christmas what was about to happen, I knew that Mama was going to walk in and not some nurse. Maybe I'd heard her heels out in the hall, or maybe I'd been wondering if she might show up even if I hadn't really wanted to let myself think about it.

But if I wasn't shocked, Mama was. She stopped halfway into the room, and for a second looked at Daddy like he was some kind of a ghost, one that maybe she'd seen before but hadn't expected to ever see again. She didn't stand still for long, though.

She walked on into the room, holding her purse real tight against her skirt, and shut the door behind her. Then she looked at me and smiled a little, or tried to. She was about to speak, but it was Michael who was brave enough to break the quiet first.

"It's good to see you, Mama," he said. "I didn't know if you'd come."

She took a good look at him and if what she saw was worse than she'd expected, she didn't let it show. I guess I thought she'd say, "Of course I was going to come," but she didn't. She just went to the side of the bed and took his hand. "I'd ask how you are," she said, "but I can see for myself."

I got up out of my chair, and I wondered what Daddy was going to do.

"Well, are you going to give your mother a hug?" she said.

I went to her and put my arms around her and she held me tightly. And while she did, I saw my father look at her, not like she was a ghost, but like he felt some great hurt inside that she reminded him of.

"How are you, Conrad?" Mama said, her voice was flat but not mean.

"All right. I thought maybe Michael could use some company, that he might want to see Seth."

"I'm glad you brought him."

He stood up then. "Why don't you take my chair?" he said.

"No, thank you. I've been driving most of the morning and I'd like to stand for a while, I think."

I went and sat down along with Daddy. Mama put her purse on the bed and started straightening up the top of the bedside table.

"Have you seen Granddaddy yet?" Michael said.

"I went by the office for a few minutes. He said to tell you he'd see you this afternoon."

"He called me and told me about Michael," Daddy said,

"which I appreciated. How has he been doing, being without your mother, I mean?"

"He's fine," she said.

Daddy looked like he was waiting to hear her say more, but she didn't speak again and the room got very quiet. The only sound was more coughing from across the hall.

"Michael," he said then, "I hope you heal quickly." He looked toward the door and stood up again. "I've got some errands I can run. Why don't I come back later, after y'all have had some time together?"

"That would be nice," Mama said, her voice still flat.

Daddy went and shook Michael's hand, then turned toward me and I saw that part of him hated he had to leave but that he knew it couldn't be any different, that maybe three of us could be in a room together, but never all four.

I got up and went to Michael's bedside, and for a minute we all just stood there, glancing at each other, then down at Michael and all of his bruises. For some reason I thought about Grandmama's funeral, how we'd all been gathered around her casket, even if Daddy couldn't sit right there with us, and how I couldn't believe she was really inside that shining silver-gray box, but I felt that day that there had been some kind of death, and later maybe I knew it was our family that had died. But standing at Michael's bed, thinking about all that we had done to each other, I didn't feel like we had died. We were just as bruised and as hurt as Michael was, but still alive if not exactly whole.

Daddy left us then, and later when he came back and picked me up, he knocked on the door and I met him out in the hall.

Not long after school started back, I went to visit Mama in Montgomery. I saw Michael too, and he told me he was going to join the navy. It was Granddaddy's idea, but Michael said he'd been thinking about it already. And maybe he was telling the truth.

He sends me postcards from the Mediterranean sometimes, and when he does, I don't think about him being in some far-off place. In my mind he is in that hospital room in Valhia with his bruises healed. We are all there, all the pieces of my family, and for one long moment I have enough strength in my arms to hold them and pull them tight against me, and then I find the strength to let them go.